BACK OFF, LADY, OR YOU'RE NEXT.

Shock and anger splintered through Cole as words in colorful crayon leaped from the piece of paper left on Margo's door. It was signed with a gold star. The killer's signature.

Cole's gaze darted to Margo again. She still looked detached and unaffected—just a police officer assessing evidence. But at the base of her throat, her pulse was throbbing. "Let me help, Margo. I can do it under the radar so I don't offend your staff."

"Cole, we've been through this. This case doesn't belong to you. Not anymore. It's mine now."

He expelled a frustrated blast of air. "At least admit you're scared. Don't pretend with me."

His statement seemed to release a rash of goose bumps, and Margo rubbed her arms to dispel them. "Okay, I'm a little unnerved. I wouldn't be human if I weren't. But give up the case? No."

He had his in. He was taking it.

LAUREN NICHOLS

From the time Waldenbooks bestselling author Lauren Nichols was able to read, there was a book in her hand—then later, in her mind. Happily, her first attempt at romantic fiction was a finalist in RWA's Golden Heart Contest, and though she didn't win, she's been blessed to sell eight romantic suspense novels, and dozens of romance, mystery and science fiction short stories to national magazines. This is her first Christian romantic suspense novel for Steeple Hill Books.

When Lauren isn't working on a project or hanging out with her family and friends, she enjoys gardening, geocaching and traveling anywhere with her very best friend, husband Mike. Lauren loves to hear from readers. You can e-mail her at lauren_nich@yahoo.com or through her Web site, www.laurennichols.com.

MARKED *for* MURDER

Lauren Nichols

Steeple
Hill®

Published by Steeple Hill Books™

STEEPLE HILL BOOKS

Steeple
Hill®

Recycling programs
for this product may
not exist in your area.

ISBN-13: 978-0-373-44402-1

MARKED FOR MURDER

Be gentle and ready to forgive; never hold grudges.
Remember, the Lord forgave you so you must
forgive others.

—*Colossians* 3:13

For Mike.
I love our life.

ONE

"Yes, I know it'll be difficult to go back to your apartment, Ms. Cortino, but you could have information that we need. I've advised one of my officers that you're on your way home now. He'll meet you there. You have our deepest sympathies on the loss of your roommate."

Margo McBride hung up the phone for what had to be the tenth time since their dispatcher went to the diner for takeout, then propped her elbows on her desk and massaged the tension headache over her eyebrows. She was about to reach for her cold coffee when the door to the Charity, Pennsylvania, police department opened... and an awkward, uncomfortable pall fell over the room. Her side of it, at least.

The tall, broad-shouldered man wearing jeans and a collarless white knit shirt didn't seem uneasy at all. He was through the low, spindled gate dividing the reception area from the office proper before Margo could blink away a sting of tears.

Cole Blackburn's wind-tossed brown hair topped rugged features and dark eyes that wanted answers.

Why today, God? Margo thought, feeling her heart break all over again. Why today, when she'd been up since 3:00 a.m. and her nerves were already raw? Then she remembered that she and God were no longer speaking, and braced herself for what was coming.

She knew why her ex-fiancé had come back.

And it wasn't for her.

Cole crossed to the gray steel desk where she'd been scanning the old Gold Star files, and spoke grimly. "Why didn't you tell me? I know it's been a long time since we spoke, but you had to realize I'd want to know about this. Why did I have to hear it on the morning news?"

Events she'd prayed would never be repeated moved through his dark eyes...a time of tragic crime photos, tearful parents and two-inch-high headlines.

"The reporter was careful not to utter the words 'serial killer,'" Cole went on, "but gold stars and strangulation tells me it's the same freak. There was a silk scarf around her neck, wasn't there? But it wasn't hers."

With a squeak of wheels, Margo rolled her swivel chair away from the desk and stood. She worked to keep her voice even and polite. "You know I can't talk about an active investigation."

"Yes, I do. But in a town of barely six thousand people, I only have to walk into the diner across the street or the convenience store down the block and I'll hear everything. Gossip flows like water around here. Unfortunately, the facts would be distorted—unintentionally, but distorted just the same. I'd rather hear the truth from you."

Maybe it was lack of sleep, or last night's horror, or his seemingly unaffected demeanor that shoved professionalism to the side. Or maybe she just needed to remind him that he wasn't the only one who'd been hurt eleven months ago. For whatever reason, she said softly, but pointedly, "And if I told you the truth? Today you'd believe me?"

Everything in Cole seemed to still as memories of their last day together stretched between them like a damaged bridge too fragile to cross. It all came back to Margo now...the bone-deep sorrow and futility of that day, the angry words. The love she'd tried so hard to preserve until she'd finally realized that the best thing she could do for the two of them was give back his ring.

Cole broke their eye contact first. Then he sighed, jammed his hands in his pockets and wandered a few feet away to regroup. His gaze skipped from the white floor tiles, to the filing cabinets and office machines, to the barely audible TV and wood-paneled walls. Margo knew what he saw there: more memories. The Officer Bill and D.A.R.E. posters taped to the paneling had hung there when Cole was part of their tiny police force. Then his dark gaze rested on the second desk in the room, and Margo felt that clawing hurt again. Once they'd shared that desk, some days sharing secret smiles, other days poring over files and desperately looking for anything that would lead them to a killer.

It hurt him to look at it, too. She could see it. But not because he missed those days with her. It hurt because the job wasn't his anymore.

Ambling back to her, he broke the heavy silence. "Who was she, Margo?" he asked quietly. "Is there someone I need to see? Someone who'd expect my condolences? I made some friends while I lived here."

Yes, he had, and she'd been one of them. His best friend, he used to say. Reluctantly, Margo walked around the desk to him. The sooner she answered his questions and he left, the sooner she could get on with the business of patching the new hole in her heart. She would not think about summer nights sitting on the tailgate of his truck, picking out constellations, or sack races at the department's picnics, or weekends cuddled together naming the babies they hoped to have one day. The past was the past. The tenderness in his dark eyes was for someone else now.

"You didn't know her. Her name was Leanne Hudson, and she was walking home from a volleyball game at the park when it happened. She was a med student who'd recently moved here with her family...small, blonde and pretty, just like the first two girls. And yes," she said, since practically every detail of the murders was already out, thanks to the teenage boys who found the body. "There was a scarf around her neck."

"But it was window dressing, wasn't it? He used his hands. And there were no defensive wounds, which suggests—as we'd thought with the other girls—that she knew her attacker or for some reason wasn't afraid of him."

"That I can't discuss." Margo drew a breath, then let it out. "There is something I can tell you, though, since you'll hear it on the street anyway. There were four gold stars on her forehead."

Shock splintered through his rugged features. "*Four?* There was no report of a third murder. I would've heard."

"There *was* no third murder. Not in this jurisdiction, anyway. We're scouring all the databases for number three, but so far—nothing."

The phone rang, and Margo murmured a polite, "Sorry, I have to take this," before she picked up the receiver.

Cole moved away to give her some privacy, his obsession with the case and his raw emotions both urgently vying for his attention. It was a close contest, but raw emotion won out. He knew it would be uncomfortable seeing her again, but he hadn't expected to feel anything beyond that. He'd been wrong. From the moment he'd walked in, memories had flown at him from every corner, making him tense and short and loading him up with guilt when he didn't have any reason to feel that way. *She* was the one who'd pulled the plug on their relationship, not him, and he refused to take the blame for it.

Cole forced himself to shift his focus—center on the killer he hadn't been able to stop, and the high-school girls who'd lost their lives in Woodland Park two years ago. Trista Morgan had been marked with one star; Missy Kennicott, two. Now he could add a third name: Leanne Hudson.

Twenty-four months ago, they'd done everything they could to nail the star-flinging freak, but with the department's limited resources, the case had dragged on for months. He'd argued repeatedly with Chief of Police John Wilcox that they needed to look elsewhere for the killer—not center solely on two carnival workers. They'd questioned and released the carneys so many times it had bordered on police harassment. But Wilcox had refused and, finally—against Margo's nervous insistence that Cole back off—he'd told Wilcox to holster his ego and bring in the Pennsylvania State Police.

Cole felt a nerve leap in his jaw and his stomach clenched. Three days later, Wilcox—with the mayor and town council's blessing—had dismissed him for insubordination, and blackballed him in surrounding counties.

Losing his job had been humiliating—life changing. Somehow he'd known even then that there would be a domino effect of trouble ahead. That's when he'd asked God to make things right again. He was the son of a deeply Christian mother and not-quite-devout dad who,

nevertheless, kept a St. Michael medal on his key ring—
St. Michael, patron saint of cops. But he'd been more like
his dad in his beliefs, and apparently the Lord had picked
up on that. It had taken him a long time to realize that he
couldn't keep treating God like some benevolent Santa
Claus when he needed a favor, then basically ignore His
existence until he needed Him again.

"So where's Wilcox?" he asked, making his way
back to Margo when she'd hung up the phone. He had
a hard time keeping the disdain out of his voice. "Out
glad-handing everybody? Assuring them that he's only
minutes away from an arrest?"

He regretted his sarcasm the moment Margo's features
softened and her gaze slid away. He knew that look.
Something had happened.

"No," she replied. "John died eight days ago of a massive heart attack."

Despite the bad blood between them, once John had
been a friend. Before the murders, he'd even been a good
cop. "I'm sorry to hear that," Cole said honestly. "How's
Adam doing?"

"As well as can be expected for a kid who just lost
his only remaining parent. I told him to contact me if he
needed anything." She nodded at the ceramic Hail to the
Chief coffee mug on the desk, jammed with pens and
pencils. "I still have to box up his dad's personal things
and take them to the house. I'm hoping he'll want to go
back to school soon. Classes started a few days ago for
the fall term. But..."

"Yeah. College has to be the last thing on his mind
right now." Cole nodded at the seat she'd vacated—John
Wilcox's padded leather chair. "You're the senior officer.
I guess you're the acting chief?"

"Yes."

Then the investigation was her headache now.

Cole released a ragged breath, finally noticing that her black-and-gray uniform was slightly rumpled, finally realizing that the wispy bangs and auburn tendrils that had escaped her loose bun weren't an attempt at fashion. Finally seeing the weary circles under her beautiful green eyes.

He was about to ask if she'd requested help from the state guys when Sarah French bustled inside, her bright red pageboy frizzing from the late-August humidity. The plump middle-aged dispatcher wore a short-sleeved, neon-green pantsuit and looked as frazzled as her hairdo.

"Margo, there's a—" She stopped abruptly, and a smile stretched her chubby cheeks. "Cole! You're back!"

Before he could offer a greeting or say he wouldn't be staying, Sarah dropped a takeout bag on her desk, raised a just-a-minute index finger and addressed Margo again. "I was leaving the diner when I saw the van pull in, so I hotfooted it over here before they barged inside. I told them to stay right where they were."

Margo sighed. "Now who's out there?"

"Channel 29 News from Johnstown—a cameraman and a pushy woman reporter."

Cole walked to the room divider. "She got pushy with you?"

Sarah slid a funky giraffe-head purse off her shoulder and set it beside her lunch. "Well…maybe I just didn't like her black eyeliner." She reached across the low barrier to hug him. "Good to see you again, honey."

"You, too, Sarah," he said, returning her hug. She'd been a staunch supporter and voice of outrage when Wilcox had fired him. He'd always appreciated that.

Sarah released him and stood back, beaming. "How's the P.I. business?"

"Like anything else. Hectic one day, slow the next."

"Which means?"

He shrugged. "It's a paycheck."

"A paycheck's good," she returned, clearly annoyed. "But you should be earning it here."

"Thanks, but it was time for me to move on."

The air beside him stirred as Margo strode past him, tucking those wispy strays back into her bun on her way to the door. Suddenly he found himself feeling sorry for her—another wrinkle he hadn't expected. And for some reason he couldn't fathom, he wanted to help. "Want me to tell them you'll have a statement later?"

She registered surprise, but only for an instant. "Thanks, but they're just doing their jobs. Every newspaper, radio and TV station within a two-hundred-mile radius has called this morning. It was only a matter of time before the vans showed up."

The phone rang again. Snatching up the receiver, Sarah spoke in a melodic singsong. "Charity Police Department. How can I direct your call?"

"Lousy way to start a new job," Cole said in an undertone.

"Yes," Margo replied.

Sarah raised a hand to stop Margo from leaving, then thanked the caller and hung up. "C.O.D.'s official," she said somberly. "The Hudson girl's hyoid bone was broken. Death by asphyxiation."

"Thanks, Sarah," Margo murmured.

Then Cole watched her square her shoulders, take a breath and go out to meet her interrogators.

Margo barely had time to adjust to the bright sunlight before a reporter in crisp white slacks and a navy blazer thrust a microphone at her. The woman's smooth chin-length hair was as black as her eyeliner.

"Chief McBride? Nancy Talbot, Channel 29 News. What can you tell us about the murder? Are there any leads?"

"First of all, it's still Officer McBride. Second, this investigation is in its infancy. It's too early for me to comment on anything. We've contacted the Pennsylvania State Police, and they're handling the evidence we've collected."

"What kind of evidence?"

"Evidence it wouldn't be prudent to share at this time."

Talbot pressed on, her voice rising. Sarah's "pushy" comment had been right on the money. "The teenage boys who found the body in the park said the victim had been strangled with a scarf. They also said there were four gold stars on her forehead. Two years ago, two young women were killed in the same park in the same way, and marked with one, then two gold stars. Does that tell us there was a third murder? Are you looking for a serial killer, ma'am?"

Great. It wasn't bad enough that the kids had blabbed; they'd blabbed to a reporter. "As I said, I'm not at liberty to answer your questions right now. I'll be releasing a statement later today."

"I appreciate your position, but the public does need answers—if for no other reason than to maintain their own safety. Some of the young women we've interviewed are frightened. The earlier victims, Missy Kennicott and Trista Morgan, were both blondes. Leanne Hudson was blonde. Shouldn't you be warning young blonde women to be extremely cautious when they walk your streets?" She thrust the mic at Margo again.

A thin crowd had begun to form outside the stone-and-timber police station, interested onlookers who'd been attracted by the news van. Across the street near the diner and municipal parking lot, people were taking their time getting into their cars.

"Ms. Talbot, we're cautioning *all* women who travel the streets after dark to be cautious. We've suggested that they walk with a friend until the situation's resolved."

"Of course," she said, quickly pressing on. "You mentioned that you've asked the Pennsylvania State Police for assistance?"

"That's correct."

She jumped on Margo's answer with both feet. "You say that as though it's standard procedure. Yet former Chief Wilcox chose to go it alone when the other two murders occurred. Should he have brought in the PSP two years ago?"

Margo didn't realize Cole had followed her outside until she felt his weighty stare and spotted him standing in the shallow crowd. He, too, appeared to be waiting for her answer.

Regret tightened her chest.

It would be so easy to say no, John Wilcox hadn't acted responsibly. Moreover, she suspected that some grudging part of Cole wanted her to state that publicly. The investigation and Cole's dismissal had marked the beginning of the end of their relationship. But answering that way would denigrate her boss's memory and cause undue pain to the families of those first two girls. With a polite smile, Margo ended the interview.

"My apologies, Ms. Talbot, but I have work to do. I *can* tell you that my department and I have made this a top priority. In fact—"

Shifting her gaze to the camera, she spoke clearly and

succinctly. "If the man—or woman—who took Leanne Hudson's life is watching, I have a message for you. We will find you. And when we do, I will personally do whatever it takes to see that you're prosecuted to the full extent of the law. There'll be no deals. You're going to pay."

"I hope you know what you're doing," Cole said gravely as they went back inside the station. They passed Sarah, who was on the phone again, scribbling something on a long pink notepad, a half-eaten sandwich and take-out drink at her elbow.

"What are you talking about?"

"I'm talking about that little speech of yours," Cole said. "You made it too personal."

"Because it *is* personal. Someone took the life of a girl this department was sworn to protect, then made sure he'd get a wagonload of publicity by mimicking an unsolved case."

She was keenly aware of him following her toward the desk she'd inherited, so close she could feel his warmth. She glanced at him briefly, thinking that conversation between them was a lot less strained when they were talking about someone or something else. "Did you see the look on that reporter's face? She found the whole thing tantalizing. She's not going to file a tragic story, she's going to sensationalize it, and we're going to have so many curiosity seekers driving through town, I'll have to deputize Sarah to keep traffic flowing."

"I don't care about that reporter. I care that you might've just made yourself a target. If the same person killed all three girls, he obviously despises women. What if he hates women in authority even more?"

"And what if Leanne Hudson's death had nothing to do with the previous murders?"

Irritation entered his tone. "I'd still tell you that com ing on like Dirty Harriet was a mistake." He fell silent for several seconds, and she could almost hear the thoughts clicking through his mind. "Are you saying you think this murder could be a copycat?"

"I don't know. We're looking at it both ways. And I wasn't trying to be Dirty Harriet."

"No?"

"No." She sank into her chair, transferred the Kenni- cott and Morgan homicide files to a drawer, then leaned her weary back into soft leather and met Cole's eyes. Suddenly, she was so exhausted, all she wanted to do was curl up in a corner and sleep for a year. "Cole, I don't have the energy to fight with you today."

"I'm not trying to start a fight. I'm merely saying that you don't have to put yourself out there the way you just did."

"Look. I don't think you understand my position. A woman at the helm of an investigation like this has to show strength. The public—especially the parents and families of those dead girls—needs to know that I'm dedicated to finding whoever did this to them. I don't want them to doubt my commitment for a second."

She was about to go on when she suddenly looked at him—really looked—and realized that beneath his brusque delivery and despite their rocky past, he *did* care about her, just a little. It was her undoing.

Margo felt the old knocking in her heart, and an emo- tional lump rose in her throat. "My heart aches for these people, Cole. That's why I'm going to use every tool at my disposal and everything I've ever learned to do my best for them. But the truth is…" She drew a breath. "The truth is, it should be you sitting in this chair. You were right. John was wrong."

For a time, the only sounds in the room were the whir of the air conditioner and the sounds of their own memories. Then the phone rang again, jarring them both.

Turning around, Sarah excused herself for interrupting. "Margo, Brett's on line one. The Hudson girl's roommate never showed up at their apartment. He wants to know if he should stick around for a while or head back here."

It took her a moment to reply. "Tell him to wait. I'll join him there in a few minutes." She looked up at Cole. "I'm sorry. I need to go."

"No problem," he said, unreadable thoughts clouding his eyes. "You have things to do. Maybe I'll drop by your place later."

Stunned, not sure why he'd do that—or if she could even handle another meeting—Margo swallowed and moistened her lips. "You're not driving back to Pittsburgh?"

"No." There was no explanation attached to the word, and she didn't think she could ask for one. Instead, she watched him leave—watched him bump knuckles with Sarah, then step into the late-August sunshine and close the door behind him.

What little energy she had left drizzled away. Why was he thinking about coming by later? What did they have to talk about? They'd said all that needed to be said eleven months ago when she'd broken their engagement. They were over.

Weren't they?

Pushing away from her desk, she said goodbye to Sarah and headed out the side door, where one of the department's two black-and-white prowl cars waited.

She slipped inside, fastened her seat belt. She couldn't think about Cole anymore—couldn't open herself up to what-ifs and maybes. Letting herself think there was hope for them would destroy her this time if it failed to happen. For her own sanity, she needed to concentrate on her job and try to ignore the nervous beating of her heart.

TWO

It was 8:20 p.m., and Margo had been running on coffee and adrenaline for seventeen hours. Pulling into her driveway, she parked the prowl car near the kitchen entry to her white cottage and sank back in her seat. She was in no hurry to get out. As she'd driven home, she'd noticed the soft lights glowing in some of the homes she'd passed, and suddenly, entering her dark, empty house wasn't very appealing.

She was thirty-two years old. She should've been married by now, maybe even had a baby on the way. She loved police work. She did. But at the end of the day, it wasn't enough. Recently, her mom had begun to guiltily suggest that it was time to let a good man into her life again. Someone like Margo's dad, who'd died after a massive stroke last year. But the truth was, no man had ever made her as happy, then as miserable, as Cole had. As for her mother... Charlotte McBride was coping better with her husband's loss now. In fact, she'd left Sunday for North Carolina to spend time with a friend who'd also been widowed. Margo found comfort in that. A year ago, her mom had been a grieving puddle of nerves, frightened of living alone, fearful of money matters, only held together with meds, her faith in God…and her only child.

Two light knocks at her car window nearly catapulted Margo through the roof. She jerked her head to the left— and her spirits fell a little further.

Cole backed up to let her out of the car. "Sorry I startled you."

"No problem," she murmured, deciding that God was just as mad at her as she was at Him. There was no other reason she could think of for Cole's wretched timing. She shut the cruiser's door and glanced around. His black Silverado was nowhere in sight. "Where did you park?"

He nodded toward the lovely Victorian bed-and-breakfast fifty yards from Margo's tiny front porch. "I walked. I'm staying at the Blackberry."

Situated on a slight hill on the opposite side of the street, it was the last building on the block before thick woods and highway asphalt took over. In the near twilight, electric candles burned in the windows of Jenna Harper's Blackberry Hill B&B, its pink shingles and white gingerbread aglow in the lamppost and landscape lighting.

Margo held back a groan. What was Jenna thinking? It was downright traitorous for a good friend to rent to another good friend's ex. Especially when it put the couple in uneasy proximity.

"You wish I were staying somewhere else," he guessed when she failed to reply.

"No, not at all," she fibbed. "I'm just…surprised."

"Good. Because I might be here for a few days. It depends."

Margo felt her nerve endings curl into little knots. "It depends on what?"

"Things," he answered cryptically, then lifted a plastic grocery bag she'd failed to notice. "Have you had dinner?"

"Yes. I had a bagel a little while ago."

His rugged features lined. "A bagel isn't dinner. You never did eat enough to keep a bird alive. Do you have eggs?"

"Cole—why do you need to know that?"

"Because I picked up a few things—ham, cheese, a green pepper. I thought if you hadn't eaten, I'd make us a couple of omelets, then we could talk about things."

"That's not a good idea."

"Why?"

Margo met his eyes. Because every time they talked she ended up hurting. "Because I've been awake since three a.m., and I can barely think. I'm tired, Cole. Too tired to fill our awkward pauses and silences. I need a shower, and I need some sleep."

"I'm only asking for a few minutes," he said. "I can have the omelets on the table by the time you're out of the shower."

She shook her head wearily. "No, you can't."

"Okay, it might take a bit longer—and you don't have to say a word. I'll do the talking. All you have to do is nod or shake your head no." He lowered his voice, his dark eyes gentle on hers. "Please. This is important to me."

Finally, Margo nodded. He'd said please. He'd said it was important. She couldn't refuse. "Can you say what you need to say in thirty minutes?"

"Yes."

Good, because that's about all she could manage.

Ten minutes later, feeling human again, Margo padded barefoot across the blue braided rug in her small living room, following the sound of music from a country station. She'd added the plants, wall hangings and other warm touches to the room. But Cole had helped her pick out her country-blue sofa and love seat, tables and lamps after she'd accepted his proposal. It was furniture she'd insisted that *she* pay for—furniture that would eventually grace the home he'd begun to build.

Months later, the only thing they'd done together was argue.

Drawing a guarded breath, Margo stepped into the kitchen. He'd said she didn't have to say a word, but that wasn't realistic. If he needed to talk, as long as he didn't bring up the past or assess blame, she'd talk back.

"You're moving right along," she said.

Cole glanced around briefly from the charcoal-gray countertop where he was adding chopped green pepper to the diced ham, onions and shredded cheese on the plate beside him. He stepped to the left and put the cutting board in the sink. "Hunger's a great motivator. I stopped at the diner a little before seven, but they were already closed. I hope Aggie's okay."

Normal conversation. So far so good.

"She's fine. She helps out with bingo at the church every other Wednesday night."

"I didn't know that," he said, taking the eggs from the fridge and setting them on the counter. He pulled a clear glass bowl from the cupboard. "I like what you've done with your kitchen."

"Thanks." Eleven months ago it had been a bright, sunny yellow. Now her oak cabinets and appliances stretched along one white wall with a burgundy-roses border. A few steps away in the dining area, a ruffled burgundy valance topped the oversize window that looked out onto her deck and the woods below. The centerpiece of burgundy silk roses, greens and baby's breath set on a doily in the middle of her round table, was her own creation.

Updating her kitchen had been therapy. She'd needed something to fill her free time after Cole left—something besides caring for her mother.

Margo stared at his broad shoulders and tapering back as he cracked eggs into the bowl and set the shells aside. And a poignant rush of déjà vu threatened to crush her heart and lungs. Once in a while after church on Sundays, they'd skip breakfast at the diner and make brunch here together. It had been quite an adventure, with both of them sidestepping and bumping into each other as they worked. He used to laugh that he couldn't wait until they moved into their dream home where they'd be cooking in a kitchen larger than a postage stamp. So much for dreams.

Cole turned around, breaking her thoughts and wiping his hands on a dish towel. His dark brown hair was longer now that he didn't have to comply with department policy. But if anything, the slightly shaggy look made him even more attractive.

"Okay, everything's ready for the pan, and your tea's decaf." He nodded at the steaming stoneware mug on the counter. "It won't keep you up."

No, but having him back in town would. "Great. Can I help?"

"Sure. Want to sauté the vegetables?"

The way she once did? Yes, she would.

The theme from an old TV detective series pounded from the cell phone clipped to Cole's belt. Pulling it from its case, he checked the number and frowned. "Sorry. I need a few minutes. It's a callback from a new client."

She hesitated. "A new client? Sounds like things are going well at Sharp."

"Well enough," he replied quietly.

They both knew what she'd meant. Are you happy there? Is the work satisfying? Do you still think about returning to your old precinct in Manhattan?

Henry Mancini's *Peter Gunn* theme continued to play in Cole's hand. "I'd better get this," he said. Then he flipped open his phone and went into the living room, his low baritone fading. "Mrs. Farley. Yes, I did call. Thanks for getting back to me."

Margo moved to the range, adjusted the flame under the skillet, added a little butter and olive oil and then tossed in the crisp vegetables.

Was he happy at Sharp Investigations? Could he be happy doing anything but police work? He'd come from a long line of tough city cops. His dad, uncles and granddad had all served, and from them had sprung a handful of rowdy cop cousins—incurable jokesters who loved saying that Cole had shed his Andy Sipowicz image to be Charity's Barney Fife.

She'd known his history when they'd fallen in love and he'd chosen to move here. She just hadn't known that being a cop was such a large part of who he was as a man. She heard his voice again, as clearly as if their first real disagreement had happened only days ago.

"You *know* Wilcox was wrong," he'd said. "I can't believe you want to stay. Is that the kind of man you want to work for?"

"Yes, he was wrong," she'd returned. "He *should've* asked for help from the state guys before the case went cold. But it doesn't make any sense for both of us to be without jobs. And if you're being honest with yourself, you know this was the first time John made a misstep."

"Yeah, John's a saint," he'd snapped, shutting her down.

After a thoughtful moment, he'd said quietly, "I spoke with my precinct captain yesterday. I can have my old job back if I want it. All I have to do is say the word."

Fear had nearly taken her breath away. "In Manhattan. Constantly putting your life on the line."

"I'd be a cop again."

"And I'd be terrified every time you walked out the door."

The nerve in his jaw worked. "What are you saying?"

"I'm saying that you're building a home we already love. And I'm saying we want children. Cole, I don't want to raise them in a city."

"I need to work, Margo. I can't go on like this indefinitely."

"I know," she'd whispered. "I'm so sorry."

They might've been able to get past that, Margo thought, pushing the ham and veggies around in the pan. But he'd grown up in a household with old-fashioned parents with old-fashioned values. The Blackburn code was simple: the husband provided for his family. Any man who couldn't hold up his end of the bargain wasn't worthy of the name.

Despite her prayers that God would send an answer, no help came, and they began to argue about everything. By the time he was offered a job with Sharp Investigations in Pittsburgh and started talking about buying a home there, she was so afraid of being uprooted and jobless if their upcoming marriage failed, she balked. Though it broke her heart, she said no again. For the time being, she would stay in Charity. She saw it as logical. He saw it as betrayal.

"It would only be temporary," she'd said. "Just until you're sure that P.I. work is what you want to do."

He'd kept tossing clothes into a suitcase. "We can't fix what's wrong between us, living apart. Whatever happened to *whither thou goest,* Margo?"

"We wouldn't be apart that often," she'd insisted. "A lot of P.I. work is done on the phone and Internet these days, and Pittsburgh is only two hours away. You could drive back any night you wanted to, and I could visit you on my days off."

That's when he'd turned around, met her eyes and said, "Fine. If you want to stay, stay. I just have one question."

"What?" she'd replied on a nervous breath.

"Are we still getting married or not?"

Blinking away the sting in her eyes, Margo moved the ham and vegetables to a plate, then slid the bowl of eggs closer, grabbed a wire whisk and put it to work.

If only he'd listened to her, and not gone head-to-head with John.

If only he'd been able to find more police work in the area.

If only her father hadn't died, leaving behind a grief-stricken wife who couldn't cope.

If only the God she'd loved and revered since her childhood hadn't ignored her prayers.

When Cole finally returned, the omelets were done—and her round resin table outside was set. "Everything's ready," she said. "I hope you don't mind. I thought we'd eat on the deck."

Cole glanced through the window, his gaze narrowing. "It'll be dark soon."

"I know. But it's pretty outside, and the mosquitoes haven't shown up yet." She couldn't very well say she felt his presence so acutely that if they ate in her tiny kitchen she wouldn't be able to swallow a bite. Outside in the evening air, she at least had a chance.

"Okay," he said amiably. "The deck it is."

The blue sky was darkening as they settled at the table and pulled in their chairs, while above the trees, a white smudge of a moon had appeared. Cole picked up the lighter she'd left on the table, lit the citronella candle between them, then set the lighter aside.

Eleven months ago, Margo with her deep connection to God, and Cole with his lukewarm faith would've joined hands and asked the blessing on their meal. Now, after too many unanswered prayers and too many losses, they simply ate, while Cole kept the conversation going and they avoided anything that approached real eye contact.

She was still picking at her food when Cole pushed his plate back, drained the last of his milk and spoke. If they'd been at a Renaissance fair, blaring trumpets would've announced to one and all that something important was coming.

His gaze drifted briefly over her damp, shoulder-length hair, gray sweats and pink T-shirt. "So, how did it go with the victim's roommate today?" he asked. "Was she helpful?"

The question was so pointed that, after their casual discussions about Charity's suddenly bustling lumber business and the friends they had in common, Margo did make real eye contact. That was when she saw the intense interest on his face. He wasn't just making idle chitchat. The Hudson girl's death was the main thing on his mind right now. That's what he wanted to talk about. *That's* why they were having omelets. His visit had nothing to do with the two of them. It was all about the case.

Slowly, she pushed her plate aside, too. "We talked about this earlier. I can't discuss it."

His earnest gaze held hers. "You can discuss it with me. I worked the case two years ago, remember?"

Of course she remembered. How could she forget? Seeing his name on the old reports she'd pulled out today had made dealing with the current case even more difficult. The files had been riddled with Cole's thoughts. Cole's handwriting. Cole's presence.

"Two years ago, I could've shared every detail with you," she said as kindly as she could. "You were on the force then."

If the reminder hurt, he didn't show it. "I won't say a word about anything you tell me. Not to anyone."

"I know that. Your discretion and integrity are two of your best qualities. You don't betray confidences."

"Then why can't we talk about this?"

"Because it's against department policy. Please don't put me on the spot." And please don't tell me you're not surprised that I said no yet again.

There was no missing the frustration in his eyes, but after a moment, he nodded.

They didn't speak for a while, just sat there listening to the sounds of night approaching. Crickets chirped beneath the deck. A slight breeze lifted the pine boughs and ruffled the maples. Peepers in the creek below sang backup to Carrie Underwood as that Louisville Slugger song drifted through the kitchen screen.

The song was nearly over when Cole eased forward,

stirred a half teaspoon of sugar into her tea, then slid it toward her. "I can help you with this case, Margo. Bring me in on a consulting basis."

As much as she hated to do it, she had to shake her head. "You know what our budget's like. We're smaller than small potatoes. There's no money. Even if there were a few dollars earmarked for consultant fees, I'd have to clear it with the mayor and town council."

His expression cooled as he asked about the man who'd officially dismissed him. "Is Hank Keller still the mayor?"

Margo shook her head again. "No, Bernice Marshall is."

"Good, then we have a shot. Tell her I'll do it for nothing. That should make her decision a lot easier."

As if it were the most natural thing in the world, he reached across the table and laced his fingers through hers. Margo felt the gentle contact all the way to that place in her heart and mind where treasured memories were stored.

His low voice pulled at her emotions. "This case cost both of us in ways I'll never forget, Margo. I need to be a part of it so I can finally close the door on that chapter of my life and move on."

He could do that? How fortunate for him. She'd never be able to close that door completely.

"Maybe you could remind Bernice that you're under-manned. With Wilcox gone, besides yourself you only have two full-time guys and two part-timers, one of whom is retirement age. We both know that some of the day-to-day work—important work—will be back-burnered while they're chasing down leads." His voice dropped a little more. "I can help, Margo."

He was right. Everything he'd said made perfect sense.

He had more experience than any other officer on the force, her included, and his instincts were spot-on. If he hadn't lost his temper with John and been dismissed, he'd be leading this investigation. She'd be taking her orders from him.

"Will you do it?"

She nodded reluctantly. Including him was a perfect solution to a lot of their problems. But there was no way the butterflies beating the walls of her stomach would agree. If this was approved, and she had no reason to think it wouldn't, they'd be working together again. Side by side. Day and night.

Cole's smile of appreciation faltered as he seemed to sense her doubts. "It'll be okay," he vowed. "We're both professionals. What we had is over. There's no reason why it has to get in the way of the work." He squeezed her hand, then withdrew his. "We got through dinner without a nuclear meltdown, didn't we?"

Yes, they had—on the surface, anyway. But they'd both steered clear of anything that could become inflammatory. That could change if emotions ran high and they started in on each other again. The answer came from a tiny voice in the back of her mind. *Then you'll have to see that that doesn't happen, won't you?*

"Okay," she said after drawing a deep breath. "I'll call the mayor first thing in the morning, and ask her to contact the council members. Considering the gravity of the situation, I doubt they'll have to meet formally. A few phone calls should do it."

Determination lined his face. "Good. I'd like to look at the Hudson file as soon as I can. The old files, too." He checked his wristwatch. "Thirty minutes. My time's up." Rising, he stacked their plates and flatware on the tray

she'd left on the seat beside him, and put their condiments and napkins back in the woven-straw basket.

"Leave them. You've done enough tonight." Had he
ever.

"At least let me do the dishes. You need to sleep."

"Yes, I do. That's why you're leaving, and why I'll
clean up in the morning." She nodded toward the steps
leading to her driveway. "Go. I'll get back to you as soon
as I hear anything."

He hesitated, then nodded. "Thank you."

"Don't thank me yet. It's not a done deal." But she
was ninety-percent sure that it would be.

"Good night, Margo. I'll talk to you soon."

"Good night."

Tears welled in her eyes as Margo watched him leave.
Then she finished clearing the table, blew out the candle
and looked toward Jenna's B&B. In the fall, when the
maples and oaks lost their leaves, she had a clear view
of the Blackberry's steep roofs and pretty turret. Now,
with the trees fully leafed, she could barely see a few tiny
lights on the second floor. That's where all the rooms
were.

That's where Cole's room would be.

Suddenly, the fear that working with him again would
send her running for a good counselor and a bottle of
antacids froze her to the deck boards. She was positively
certifiable. What on earth had she been thinking when
she agreed to this?

You know, that tiny voice in her head whispered. *You
know, and you don't want to admit it.*

She was still upset twenty minutes later when the
cordless phone on her nightstand shrilled. Margo bolted
upright in bed.

Quickly clicking on her lamp, she grabbed the phone and hoped with all her heart that it wasn't more bad news. Then she checked the caller ID and stilled. It wasn't Steve O'Dell at the station. Cole's cell phone number glowed in the display window.

Taking a deep breath, then clearing her throat, she said hello.

"It's me," he said.

"I know. Caller ID. Did you forget something?"

"Yes and no. I've been thinking about that interview of yours. You threw down the gauntlet today—practically issued a challenge to the killer. I just want to remind you to be more aware of your surroundings. I was standing outside your car for at least ten seconds before I rapped at your window, but you didn't know I was there."

What did she say to that? It was your fault because I was thinking about you? That wouldn't be wise. "I was distracted."

"I could see that. But from now on, you can't afford to be." He hesitated again. "Be careful, okay?"

"I will. Thanks for calling."

He waited on the line through the uncomfortable pause, then said, "Well…good night again."

"Good night," she returned quietly.

Margo replaced the handset in its cradle, then, after a longing look at the Bible beside the phone, flopped back on her pillow. Tomorrow would be another difficult day, and she needed to be clearheaded to deal with it. She needed to sleep. More than that, she needed to forget about the tall, tanned, dark-haired man who'd suddenly dropped back into her life. As if that was an option.

She started to turn off her bedside lamp again, then paused to look at the clock. She knew Bernice Marshall, knew she generally stayed up to watch the late news. Sighing, she picked up the phone again.

"Bernice?" she said when the woman answered. "It's Margo. Are you wearing your mayor's hat? I need a favor."

He squatted in the ferns and pine needles, breathing in the fecund scents of pine, damp earth and blackberries. The remaining berries were on their way to wine now, but the tangy-sweet scent still lingered. He glared at the house—felt the hatred bubble up inside of him as he watched a light go off again upstairs.

She thought she was hot stuff. Thought she was so superior. Thought she could scare him with threats and warnings, and that utterly pathetic impression of a steely-eyed stare. He fingered the folded sheet of paper in his pocket, although he couldn't really feel it. Not through the plastic bag and his latex gloves.

Satisfied that no one could see him, he sprang nimbly to his feet, then made his way through the thick firs and maples toward the creek that bisected the town. It was time *he* issued a warning.

Stupid woman.

She had no idea who she was playing with.

THREE

Cole Blackburn sat in the dark on the second-floor turret porch, listening to the party going on a quarter mile away in a clearing local teens had named and claimed. The inn was the last building on the block, so he could even see the faint glow of a fire against the night sky. When he'd worn a badge here, he'd shagged kids out of the "party place" on more than one occasion.

But that wasn't the reason he couldn't sleep tonight.

His gut clenched as his thoughts spun back to Margo. She was a good cop, and more than qualified to handle the top position. But she was a woman, and no matter how Stone Age his thinking was, he didn't want her involved in this mess. Not that he was still in love with her. She'd taken a veritable scalpel to that emotion when she'd given back his ring.

Frowning, he sipped from a bottle of cranberry something-or-other that he'd found in the small fridge in his room.

He'd known she'd needed to be with her mother after her dad died. That was a given; she was a devoted daughter—probably because Frank and Charlotte McBride had been one of the most devoted *couples* he'd ever met. Love grows from love. Frank had been the head of the family, making decisions, taking care of the bills, single-handedly managing their finances. Charlotte had created a warm, loving home. When Frank's death threw her into a world she wasn't prepared for, Margo became her fiscal and emotional lifeline. He'd understood and agreed to postpone their wedding and Margo's move to Pittsburgh until Charlotte had a handle on her grief.

Cole stared out at the dark sky alive with stars.

But when months passed with Charlotte making no attempt to stand on her own two feet, he'd had to say something. He'd done it badly, but the words had had to be said.

He'd told Margo she was enabling her mother, and nothing was going to change until she stopped being a crutch. He'd wanted to can the big, fancy wedding, find Reverend Landers and start their married life together. He was tired of being last on her list. First she chose to stay on the job, then she balked at the move to Pittsburgh, then her dad died and she wanted to postpone the wedding again. He deserved better, he'd told her. She'd cried and handed back his ring. That's when he found out what all the excuses and delays really meant.

Cole took a long swig of his cranberry-whatever to combat the dull ache in his chest.

She'd wanted out.

Down the road, heavy metal gave way to moody saxophone tones and stirring lyrics. And against Cole's will, Richard Marx's "Endless Summer Nights" took him back to another night like this one. One clear, moonlit mid-July night, after he'd moved to Charity. They'd gone to Payton's Rocks, a huge tumble of boulders and high grasses two miles from the town limits.

Far from the lights of town, they'd sat on his truck's tailgate, and gazed in awe at the heavens. He'd never seen stars like that before—billions upon billions of them shimmering in an ink-black sky that stretched farther than his mind could ever comprehend. He'd felt small and insignificant that night, humbled in the presence of God's universe.

That's how large his love for her had been back then. Back when he was first in her life, not last in a long string of other people and other commitments.

Suddenly a police cruiser with lights flashing sped up the street and appeared to swerve into Margo's driveway down the block. Bolting to his feet, Cole craned his neck past the weeping willow tree in the B&B's front yard to be certain. His heartbeat skyrocketed. An officer was getting out of the prowl car and rushing up Margo's front steps.

Her motion lights went on, followed by her porch light.

There was only one reason for a patrolman with lights flashing to go to his chief in the middle of the night, and it wasn't because a bunch of kids were partying. There'd been more trouble.

Cole flew pell-mell downstairs and out the door. He raced for that porch light, glad he'd had the presence of mind to pack a small duffel. If he looked like an idiot wearing gray sweats with cowboy boots, he didn't care.

He could see the two of them now, through the screen door. The interior door had been left open.

He slowed as he reached the sidewalk, knowing that Margo wasn't going to like this, knowing that he was overstepping. But the need to know what had happened was strong, and he climbed the porch steps. Hopefully by midday tomorrow, he'd have official standing in the investigation.

His leather soles scraped on the gritty concrete. Apparently, they heard it, too.

Margo's eyes widened for a second and then, lips thinning, she excused herself and stepped out on the porch. She spoke in an undertone. "Sometime you'll have to tell me how you knew about this."

"Are you asking me to leave?" he replied in the same low voice.

"No, but you need to give me a few minutes." She nodded at the padded redwood chairs on her lattice-trimmed porch. "Pick one."

Then she went back inside and shut both doors.

They opened again a few minutes later, and she beckoned him inside. The familiar second set of eyes he encountered didn't look pleased to see him.

"Steve," she said to her officer, "I think you remember Cole."

O'Dell should remember him, Cole thought, though they'd never been formally introduced. O'Dell had taken his place two years ago, after Wilcox gave him the ax.

The husky patrolman with the ruddy complexion nodded, but the lips beneath his red brush of a mustache didn't smile, even when he offered his hand.

Cole shook it, guessing O'Dell's age at somewhere around forty. He had a strong grip and thick fingers, and though his stiff expression had cracked a little, Cole knew he and O'Dell weren't going to hit it off—probably because he saw Cole as the intruder he was.

If Margo had picked up on the tension, she didn't react to it. "Since Cole worked the original Gold Star case, he'll be coming aboard tomorrow as a consultant. I spoke to Bernice a little while ago," she added when Cole raised a questioning brow. "She doesn't see a problem."

She turned to O'Dell again. "Okay," she said. "Let's back up and start again for Cole's benefit."

O'Dell pulled a plastic evidence bag from his pocket. It contained a folded sheet of typing paper with a piece of masking tape attached to it.

"As I said, I'd just finished some paperwork and was heading out to shut down the party place when I saw the note. Charlie had told the kids earlier that it was lights and fire out by midnight." He indicated the evidence bag. "Someone taped it to the door while I was occupied." O'Dell's lips thinned. "Looks like it was meant for you."

Cole studied Margo's face. She never flinched. She just led them to the kitchen table, opened the bag, grasped the note by the very tip of one corner and eased it out. She shook it open on the table.

Shock and anger splintered through him as words in colorful crayon leaped from the page.

BACK OFF, LADY, OR YOU'RE NEXT.

It was signed with a gold star.

Cole's gaze darted to Margo again. She still looked detached and unaffected—just a police officer assessing evidence. But at the base of her throat, her pulse was throbbing.

She tucked the note back in the evidence bag just as cautiously as she'd retrieved it, then turned to O'Dell. "Okay. Photograph it, make a detailed note for our files, then run this over to the state-police barracks. Their lab will take it from here."

Cole trailed behind them as she walked O'Dell to the front door. "He probably wore gloves when he wrote it, but if we're lucky, maybe he got sloppy and left a print on the masking tape. Did you dust the door?"

"I will when I get back. I thought it was more important to get this to you."

She nodded. "I'll call and let them know you're coming. See you in a few hours."

When the prowl car had pulled out and Margo had spoken to the PSP, she hung up the phone and walked back to Cole. She was dressed in her sweats and pink T-shirt again, and that pulse in her throat was still moving along at a steady clip. Her hair hung long and silky around her shoulders.

"Now," she said wearily. "What are you doing here? Are you stalking me?"

He guessed that depended on her definition of *stalking*. He preferred to think of it as watching over her. "No, I was sitting on the porch when O'Dell flew up the road and pulled into your driveway. Obviously, there'd been some trouble."

He tried to ignore the ball of fear in his stomach. "That was pretty bold of our friend, taping that note to the door. You need to take a few precautions. Is there a chance Sarah could move in with you for a while?"

She looked at him as though he'd suddenly grown two heads. "I'm not going to ask Sarah to move in. I'm a police officer and I carry a gun. Guns trump scarves. I don't need a babysitter, Cole."

"All right, but at least admit you're scared. Don't pretend with me."

His statement seemed to release a rash of goose bumps, and Margo chafed her hands over her arms. "Okay, I'm a little unnerved. I wouldn't be human if I weren't. But I'm not going to run around like Henny Penny screaming that the sky is falling. Besides," she went on, "there's a chance that note *could* be a prank. From the level of news coverage we've been getting, half the state knows what's going on here."

She locked her pretty green gaze on his. "But if the note *was* from the killer, he might've given us a partial print or enough DNA evidence for an arrest. In fact," she said, her voice gaining conviction, "if I press the issue he might get ticked off enough to write again. We both know that an angry criminal is a careless criminal."

Frustrated, Cole released a blast of air. "Are you listening to yourself? Putting yourself at risk to prove you can do the job just as well as a man—"

"I'm not doing that!"

"Aren't you? It sure looks that way to me."

They glared through a dozen ticks of the living room's wall clock, both of them refusing to look away. Then something unfathomable happened. The room seemed to shrink, and the air in it seemed to thin, taking Cole to the point of light-headedness. Memories he'd been trying to keep at bay filled his mind and heart. And if his cop's instincts were working even a little, he saw those same memories cloud Margo's eyes.

Lifting his hand, he moved a long auburn strand that had become caught in her eyelashes...tucked it aside. Then his voice dropped so low he barely recognized it. "I know I don't always choose my words wisely. But we meant something to each other once, Margo. Even though we messed it up, that still counts with me. I'm afraid for you. Can't you see that?"

"Yes," she returned in a whisper that just about put him away. "Yes, I can."

"Then you're not mad?"

She shook her head. "No. I'm not mad."

And they were lost.

The kiss was warm and soft and bittersweet, and so full of memories and yearning for what might've been that it broke Margo's heart. Once they'd had a love so special, her every prayer had included her thanks to God for bringing them together. Back then there had been no sadness in their kisses, only love, and laughter and a boundless faith in their future. But as the kiss went on, a smidgen of hope filtered through the hopelessness, and Margo's rock-bottom spirits began to lift a little. Maybe it wasn't too late for them. Maybe he was ready to forgive—

Cole broke the kiss and retreated to the opposite corner of her tiny living room, his expression a mixture of self-derision and apology. "I'm sorry," he said. "I shouldn't have done that. I guess we're both a little unhinged tonight."

Margo fought for balance, fought to hide her disappointment, grappled for her dignity. It took her a full moment to speak. The warm sensation of his lips on hers was fading now, replaced by cool air and regret.

"It's just the case," she replied quietly. "Apparently, old habits *do* die hard." She took them back to the conversation that had precipitated that kiss. "Thank you for caring, though. I won't hire a nanny, but I will be cautious."

Cole's somber reply made her feel even worse. "I've always cared, Margo."

Maybe he had, she thought. He just hadn't cared enough. If he had, he would've believed her when she'd told him she loved him.

"Well," he said, casting about before turning toward the door. "I'd better get back and let you get some sleep. Are your doors and windows locked?"

She nodded. All except the inside and screen doors,

and they soon would be. How quickly they'd leaped from tenderness to all-business again.

"He won't bother me tonight. He wants me to think about the note for a while, otherwise it defeats the purpose of sending it. What I don't understand is, why did he write it? Do I make him nervous? Do I have information I'm not aware of?"

"I don't know. I've been wondering the same thing." Cole stepped out on the porch, where a squadron of moths bumped and fluttered against her porch light. "I won't go to the station in the morning. I know you'll need time to let everyone know I'm coming aboard. But I'd appreciate sitting down with you soon, so you can fill me in."

She eased against the door frame. "We'll do it tomorrow." But there was something she needed to get straight with him. Steve O'Dell had accepted the fact that an ex-officer with more experience than he had would be helping out. But he wasn't happy. "Cole, I need to say something, and I hope you won't misunderstand."

"Go ahead."

"I know how important this is to you. But I also know how you act when you get up a full head of steam. Especially when you know you're right. Promise me that you'll remember you're only consulting. I don't want you trampling some very competent officers on your way to an arrest."

From the expression on his face, he knew she was referring to his clash with John Wilcox.

"Wouldn't dream of it. I'll deal only with you, and you'll call the shots." Sending her an overly polite smile, he turned to leave. "It'll be your way or the highway."

It was a clichéd, overused quip, but it was also a subtle

nod to their past. At least he hadn't added, *You know. The way it's always been.*

Margo said good-night and closed the door. So much for her hope that they could let sleeping dogs lie.

The dogs were up and they were barking up a storm.

By 5:00 a.m., after four hours of tossing and turning and hearing every chirping bird in the neighborhood greet the dawn, Margo showered and drove to the station. Steve O'Dell was just climbing into the prowl car, preparing to make his final rounds before his shift ended.

"You're here early," he said through the open car door.

"I know. I couldn't sleep." Margo ascended the three concrete steps to the door and found the office key on her crowded ring. "How'd it go with the PSP? Any problems?"

"Nope."

"Good." She unlocked the door. "Any coffee left?"

His blue gaze turned to ice. So did his tone. "Sorry. I wasn't expecting you for another hour or so."

Margo hesitated for several seconds, wondering if this was about bringing Cole into the investigation, or something else. Steve could be testy, but the two of them had always had a good working relationship. Then again, maybe he was as tired and wired as she was, and thought—rightly so—that coffee wasn't a priority. "That's okay," she said. "I'll make us a fresh pot. See you when you get back."

"Yeah. See you in a little while."

Margo waved as he drove off, then let herself inside, dropped her shoulder bag on her desk and went to work. She crossed to the bank of filing cabinets and pulled out the Kennicott, Morgan and Hudson folders, then headed for the copy machine at the rear of the office. Feelings of disloyalty dogged her steps as she wondered how everyone else would feel about Cole's inclusion. But they needed to find a killer before he struck again.

Twenty minutes later, copies of the old and new Gold Star files were in an oversize envelope in her cruiser. She was ready to leave again when Steve returned at 6:10.

"I have to step out for a half hour or so," she said, "but I glanced at your notes. Dusting the door was a waste of time, huh?"

"Unfortunately." He went to the coffeemaker and filled his cup. "The area on and around the latch was full of prints, but they were smeared and I'm guessing that most of them were ours. As for the rest... Sorry, boss, there was nothing on the door where I found the note. Not even a smudge."

Boss? Margo stilled. He'd called her *boss*. Maybe she'd been too quick to dismiss the chilly look he'd sent her. Maybe it had nothing to do with being tired, *or* with Cole. Maybe it had more to do with pecking order. O'Dell was forty—eight years older than she was—but he didn't have as many years in law enforcement. Still, if he felt he deserved the acting-chief position, that could account for his testiness. She decided that now wasn't the best time to mention that she'd copied a set of files for Cole.

Resting her hand on the doorknob, she spoke quietly. "Steve, I know things have changed around here, but I'm still Margo. Please don't call me boss." Until John's death, even though she'd been the senior officer, she, Steve, Brett and part-timers Charlie Banks and "Fish" Troutman had pretty much worked at the same level and shared the same jobs. Sure, there'd been a few disagreements, but they'd been minor and easily smoothed over. Things were different now, however, and suddenly she wasn't sure how everyone felt about it.

He seemed to read her mind. "Worried about a mutiny?" he asked, stirring cream into his coffee.

She took a second to answer. "Should I be?"

Smiling, he waved off her concerns. "Nah. We're a team, right? Someone has to answer to the mayor and the media. You're the senior officer. I'm just glad it's not me."

"You're sure? Because if there's a problem we need to talk about it."

"I'm positive. Relax. We're good."

"Whew," she replied jokingly, then opened the door. "Put your feet up and veg for a while. I'll be back before Sarah and Brett come in."

Still, that niggling feeling that things weren't as okay as he said stayed with her.

The Blackberry Hill B&B was a busy place at 6:20 a.m. A smiling older couple was just getting into their car, while on the wraparound porch, two women sat flipping though travel brochures and sipping coffee. Margo strode inside and made her way through the hardwood foyer to the dining room.

Jenna Harper was clearing away place settings on two of her four lace-and-glass-covered round tables, the chink of silverware and the wonderful aromas of coffee and blueberry muffins riding the air.

Lovely rose swags and a variety of Victorian prints adorned the cream-and-roses wallpaper, while doilies, dolls and antiques added warmth and charm to the room.

Jenna's welcoming smile fell like a stone. Setting a

creamer down, she crossed the floor to Margo. "Are you all right?"

Jenna was five feet, seven inches of dark blond class with a slender figure, a light garden tan and—usually—a warm smile. Today, she wore white slacks topped by a white gauze tunic and turquoise-and-coral beads.

Margo winced. "Do I look that bad?"

"No, but your dark circles are getting dark circles. Let me get you some breakfast. Some coffee, at least."

"Thanks, but I'm really pressed for time this morning. I need to see one of your guests."

Jenna tipped her head curiously. "Well, since you had to have passed four of them on your way in, and I only had five guests last night, I guess you mean your ex."

When Jenna had returned to Charity eight months ago, they'd each shared bits of their pasts, but she'd never shown Jenna a snapshot of Cole, and she doubted she'd ever mentioned his last name. Then again, as she and Cole had agreed yesterday, people in small towns loved to talk.

"How did you—"

"Easy. How many Cole Blackburns could there possibly be? Especially one who looks like he does. Besides..." she said with a touch of worried hesitance, "you know how I feel about renting to single men. No references, no room. He had a good one."

"Me."

"Yes." Folding her arms across her chest, Jenna went on quietly. "So, are you two on again?"

Margo expelled a flat laugh. "No. Not the way you mean, anyhow. As they say in every film I've seen lately, it's complicated. Can you buzz his room?"

"I could, but he wouldn't answer. He left a few minutes ago. I'm surprised you didn't pass him on the way."

"Oh? Did he say where he was going?"

"Yes, back to his place."

Margo felt her jaw drop. After all his persistence—
"He went back to Pittsburgh?"

"Yes, but only to grab fresh clothes and finish up some work."

"Then…you're holding his room?"

"Uh-huh. He asked about WiFi, and I told him that yes, we're set up for the Internet, so I guess he's planning to do some work from here." Jenna paused, her head tilting curiously. "You're disappointed."

"No, not really. I'm just—" Margo released a breath, frustrated. "The truth is, I have no idea how I feel, and right now I don't have time to sort it out."

Jenna snagged Margo's hand and led her to a corner table where white carafes and pots of strawberry and peach preserves were clustered. "Sit. Let's talk."

Margo shook her head. "You don't know how badly I want to, but I have to go."

"Not until seven, which means you can stay for at least a half hour. Three of my guests are gone, and the two women on the porch have already eaten. If they want croissants or more coffee, there's a cordial table out there."

"I really can't," Margo returned. "It would take me a week to explain, and unfortunately… Well, you know what's going on."

Jenna spoke softly. "The Hudson girl. How tragic."

"Yes. Can we get together in a day or two? Hopefully, I'll have some time by then."

"Of course," Jenna replied, her concern deepening. "Just give me a call. Or show up. I'm always here."

Yes, she was—day in, night out. "We need to talk about that, too, sometime. You should get out more."

"I do. I go to the grocery store, I go to church and occasionally I even have lunch with my good friend Margo or take in a movie."

"You know that's not what I mean," Margo returned gently.

Jenna smiled. "I know. But it's all I can handle right now."

They were a pair, Margo thought as she left that manila envelope in Cole's room, then drove off. If things didn't change, neither of them would ever again have a life that included the male of the species.

Seven hours later, she'd finished an enlightening phone conversation with an officer from a neighboring county, and was preparing to leave when Cole strode into the office. He was all broad shoulders and narrow hips in faded jeans and a navy polo shirt. Margo drew a stabilizing breath.

"Can you get away for a few minutes?" he asked.

"Actually, I'm on my way out the door right now," she replied. Part-timer Charlie Banks, who was now racking up full-time hours, was talking on the phone trying to track down a man Leanne Hudson had been seeing, but so far, no luck. Chase Merritt—whom Hudson's roommate, Ellie Cortino, had identified—seemed to have dropped off the face of the earth. They'd questioned the volleyball team yesterday, and now Brett was at the park, interviewing two teenage employees who'd been out of town when the murder occurred. And dear Sarah was handling yet another call from the media. The office was covered.

Margo came around her desk. "You found my gift?" Everyone knew about Cole's involvement now. And like always, supportive Sarah, Charlie and Brett, who'd also worked with him, were all for it.

"Yes. Thank you."

"Good. Just let me grab my sunglasses and let the troops know where I'll be for the next few hours. Then I'll see you outside."

Cole narrowed his gaze. "Where *will* you be?"

She started to say she'd tell him later when the door opened again and an angry young man blew inside.

FOUR

Cole stepped to the side as Adam Wilcox stormed past Sarah's desk, came through the spindled gate and made a beeline for Margo's desk. He'd changed since he'd gone to college, filled out. The thin boy with acne and glasses was gone, replaced by a good-looking kid in a red T-shirt and khakis. His light brown hair was streaked with blond now, and contact lenses made his eyes appear bluer than usual. Cole had considered seeing Adam sometime today to offer his condolences, but he wasn't sure his sympathies would be welcomed.

The kid's churning gaze bounced off Cole as he approached Margo, but he didn't smile and he didn't acknowledge Cole's nod.

"Thanks a lot, Margo," he said, locking his eyes on hers. "Thanks a whole lot."

Cole watched Margo's expression move from surprise to confusion. "Adam," she said. "What's wrong?"

His anger was nearly palpable, but so was his grief. His voice rose. "What's wrong? I just saw the interview you gave that Johnstown reporter. I was talking to an insurance guy on the phone, and all of a sudden, there you were on TV practically saying my dad bungled the first Gold Star murders. How could you do that to him? How could you do it to *me?*"

It was Cole's turn to be confused. Margo had been nothing but diplomatic and respectful. He saw Sarah turn in her chair, saw portly Charlie Banks hang up the phone and stand sentinel, ready to help if things got sticky. Still, the shaggy gray brows above his blue eyes had dipped low in sympathy.

"Adam," Margo said, "I would never insult or disrespect your father. You must have misunderstood."

"I didn't misunderstand anything. You should've told that woman flat out that my dad didn't need to call in the state police. He knew who killed those girls. He just couldn't put him away. You made him look clueless."

Cole watched Margo move closer, her tone gentle and sincere. "Adam, your dad was a great cop. I would never say or do anything to denigrate his memory. If it sounded that way, I'm deeply sorry." She signaled Sarah. "Let me get you some coffee or a soft drink, then we can go back to the interrogation room, sit down and talk this through. Okay?"

He shook his head no. Then tears welled in his eyes and he blinked and looked away. "I'm sorry," he said. "It's been a lousy week."

"I know," she said softly.

"I'm alone now."

Sarah's pudgy face lined in sympathy, then following Charlie's lead, she went back to work. Cole walked to Charlie's desk, a desk he'd used frequently, giving Adam and Margo some space to talk quietly.

Banks was a heavyset, grandfatherly man with rimless bifocals, a gray walrus mustache and a heart of gold, but the trademark gruffness in his voice always made him sound as if he was half ticked off. He stood to shake Cole's hand.

"Hey, Charlie," Cole said. "You're looking well."

Charlie gripped his hand hard and long. "You too, Cole. Good to see you. Sarah said you came in yesterday."

"Yeah. I heard one of the initial reports and got interested."

"I'm not surprised. You doin' okay in Pittsburgh?"

"Fair to middling, as they say. How's your family?"

"Good. Doris and I got another grandbaby on the way. Real quick now—just a matter of days. Sad thing is, it's our Ginny's first, and her husband's over there in Afghanistan." He nodded a few times. "But we're here for her. We'll help her get this baby born."

"You're good parents," Cole said. "Congratulations."

"Thanks. We try." Charlie's gaze shifted to the conversation going on near Margo's desk. "That's a bad situation over there," he said quietly. "Young kid, both parents gone, no sisters or brothers. John's sister and her husband want the boy to move in with them, but Adam's of age now, and he wants to stay at the house."

"It's his home," Cole said, a shrug in his voice. "I don't know about you, but I'd feel the same way. His life's already been turned upside down." He watched Margo dump the pencils and pens out of that Hail to the Chief mug and hand it to Adam. Watched the kid hug her for a long time. Then, surprising Cole at the brevity of their conversation, Margo walked him through the gate and out the door.

When she came back inside a minute later, she exhaled, spoke to Sarah, then crossed to Cole where he stood with Charlie. "I'll see you outside. I need to talk to Charlie before I leave."

Presently, with Charlie and Sarah apprised of her plans, Margo descended the steps, and crossed the sidewalk to Cole where he waited beside his parked truck. High above them, the midday sun shone down, baking the concrete beneath their feet. The August air was stone still, heavy with humidity.

Cole pushed away from the side of his truck. "Are you all right? Your talk with Adam got a little intense."

"I'm fine. I just wish he was." She brushed a few wispy strands back from her face. "I just hope he'll go back to school. He said there's a special girl there, and friends. He needs them now."

"He's decided against it for certain?"

"No, but he's leaning toward skipping this semester and enrolling for the spring term."

He nodded. "You were good with him in there."

"Thanks, I tried." She drew a breath and changed the subject. "Now, what did you want to tell me?"

"Just that Burgess and Tate Amusements is back in the area. They're only forty-five miles away at—"

"—the Laurel Banks carnival grounds," Margo finished. "I know. I just got off the phone with the Laurel Banks P.D."

Cole's brow lined. "Trouble?"

"Not so far, but they generally check out licenses and pay a few courtesy calls when carnivals and other amusements come to town. Guess what? The men we questioned two years ago are still working for them." Margo slipped on her sunglasses. "And of course, they're both still pillars of the community. One just served time for aggravated assault and the other's behind in his child support payments. How did you find out they were nearby?"

"By accident," he said wryly. "You know, the way all good investigative work is done. When I was driving back from Pittsburgh, I stopped for coffee at a convenience store and saw a carnival poster. It wasn't the Burgess and Tate company, but it made me think that a higher power wanted me to see that sign. I looked up B and T's home-base phone number on the Internet and got their summer route and hours."

She had to grin. "The man's a detective."

He grinned back. "Duly licensed and everything." Their gazes held for a few seconds, fond memories seeming to float between them. Then Cole glanced away and went on. "Anyway, even though we didn't like them for the first two murders, it's a pretty big coincidence when the ride jockeys show up again just as another young woman is killed."

"It certainly is. That's why I'm heading over there right now."

He seemed to digest that for a half second, then said, "What a coincidence. So am I."

Margo's smile went south. "Oh, no, you're not. I appreciate your help, but you're staying behind the scenes. An officer from the LBPD is meeting me there. I'll call you later and let you know how things went."

"Well…no."

She blinked in shock. "No?"

"Sorry, but I'm a private citizen who suddenly has a real yen for a candy apple. As far as I know, the only place I can get one is at the Burgess and Tate carnival. I figure it's going on four o'clock now, so I can be there just before they open at five."

Glaring, Margo closed the distance between them

until they were toe-to-toe. "If you go off half-cocked and jeopardize this investigation in any way, I will lock you up and throw away the key."

"I have no intention of doing that. I told you. I just want a candy apple." He opened the truck's passenger-side door. "Want to save on gas and ride with me? Car pooling's big now. The nation's going green."

Some days there were simply no words to describe him. *Infuriating* came close. How could a man who looked that good be such a colossal pain in the rump? Okay. There was nothing she could do to keep him from his candy apple. But they were *not* leaving here together.

"This is police business, not a joyride," she said, turning away and heading for her cruiser. She paused for a final word as she opened the door. *"Behave."*

"Don't I always?"

No, he didn't. Margo climbed inside and shut him out. If he had, he'd still be on the force, and they'd be married by now.

The sprawling carnival was a maze of tents and rides, bright primary colors and shimmering flags, all set up in a vacant dirt-and-grass field on the outskirts of town. As Cole had guessed, he and Margo pulled into the grassy parking area twenty minutes before fun city opened for the evening. They weren't the first to arrive. Quite a few carnival-goers were already here, some milling about, others waiting in their parked cars. Happy chatter came from kids in the backseats.

One last hurrah before the elementary school opened next week.

Cole parked his black Silverado beside Margo's cruiser, then swung out and walked around the truck to join her. He glanced about. No sign of the LBPD yet— just a few volunteer firemen hanging around to keep people from parking sideways. It bothered him that the officer wasn't here. He didn't want her going it alone with those cretins, especially after last night's note.

Margo got out of the car and hit the door locks and, unrepentant chauvinist that he was, Cole took a minute to enjoy the view. She was dressed in the same black-and-gray uniform he'd once worn, but there was nothing remotely masculine about her. She was all woman, and she was beautiful. But he'd never be a fan of the twirled auburn knot at the back of her head.

"What?" she said, catching him looking.

"Nothing."

"No, you were thinking something. What?"

"Okay," he replied, falling into step beside her. She'd set her sights on the house trailers behind the rides, ostensibly because she might find the manager back there. "I was wondering if that bun of yours gives you a headache."

Her brow knit curiously. "No, why?"

"Because it gives me one," he grumbled. "You have pretty hair. You should wear it down." Before she could tell him that her hairstyle was no longer any of his business, he said, "So, where's the cop who was supposed to meet you?"

"He's not coming. Sarah radioed me a few minutes ago. He went out on a domestic disturbance call that ended in an arrest. He'll be a while processing the guy."

Maybe that was good news. "Okay, I'll be your backup."

He got the expected reply. "I don't need a backup. I'm just going to ask those two thugs a few questions and head back to Charity." She stopped before the roped-off entrance where a sign said the carnival was closed. She apparently realized he planned to follow her to the trailers. "Uh-uh. This is as far as you go." A tiny smile flitted across her lips. "Find something to do until the candy-apple stand opens."

Cole made a face, then waited until she'd dipped under the rope and was on her way before he said to himself, "Thank you, Acting Chief McBride. I'll do that."

Straight ahead of him, three lines of concession stands and flat store games were interspersed with the hanky panks, alibi joints and a few kiddie rides. Dirt and trampled-grass aisles ran parallel between them. A bit farther back, the Bullet scraped the sky, along with a half-dozen other cranking, popping, whirling rides designed to make people nauseous. Cole focused on one ride only.

The carousel.

He dipped under the roped-off entrance just as lively music began to spill from loudspeakers and carneys headed for their stations and booths. Others were already there, stoking up their grills and deep fryers, and layering the air with great, greasy food smells. The guy at the cotton-candy booth gave him the stink eye as he walked past, but didn't attempt to turn him back. Maybe because he'd spotted Cole with Margo and made some assumptions. Or maybe Cole still had his cop walk. He suspected that a lot of these guys had seen that walk before, a few of them up close and personal.

The graying ride jockey wearing snug jeans and a tight purple T-shirt over his bulging muscles knew Cole's walk well.

He walked up to the motionless carousel as Ray Masters exited the ride's fancy mirrored core, carrying a wrench. Cole took a moment to meet the man's deadeye stare, then stepped up onto the platform. Except for a palomino or two, the horses were still the scary-ugly creatures he remembered from his childhood.

Masters hooked a hand on a brass pole and leaped nimbly onto the boards. He was in his mid-forties, ripcord lean, and—no surprise—oozed attitude and entitlement, just as he had two years ago. He was an inch shorter than Cole's six-foot-two frame.

"Well, well. Officer Blackburn, isn't it? It's been a while since you came by to harass me. What took you so long this time?"

Cole wondered about Masters's reference to the new crime, then shook off the thought. If Masters had been anywhere in the vicinity of a TV or a radio, he knew. "I never harassed you, Masters. I just asked a few civil questions and you gave me a few snotty answers. Probably the same answers I'll get this time, but I'd like to give it a shot anyhow. You apparently know about the latest murder. So where were you while some other scum ball was killing one of our local girls?"

He sent Cole a slow, sarcastic smile. "I was playing pinochle with my friend Arnie. You remember Arnie, right?"

"How could I forget? Shaved head, gold tooth and thirty earrings, all duded up in biker-black. Pleasant guy. Sullen and antagonistic were his two best qualities. I don't suppose he's around?"

A feminine voice he hoped he wouldn't hear quite this soon broke in.

"Yes, he is. And I'll be speaking with him as soon as I've finished with Mr. Masters."

Cole turned around to see Margo behind him. She

smiled, but the look in her eyes told him to back off and let her do her job.

"Found the manager already?" he replied cheerfully.

"Actually, he found me, halfway to the trailers. He couldn't contact Mr. Masters on *his* cell phone, but he did reach Mr. Shanks and told him I'd be seeing him at the Tilt-a-Whirl." Her gaze flicked to Masters as she pulled a notebook and pen from the pouch on her belt. "I understand the carnival will be opening in the next few minutes so let's do this fast, before you and Mr. Shanks can put your heads together and come up with a bestseller. Where were you between the hours of eleven o'clock on Tuesday, August 20, and two a.m. August 21?"

Masters glanced between the two of them, then smiled again as he appeared to figure out who had the power here—and who didn't. "I already told your *boy,* here," he said, chuckling when Cole countered with a bored stare. "I was playing pinochle."

Margo sent Masters a withering look. "I don't suppose anyone without a criminal record can verify that?"

"Of course."

"How about last night between the hours of eleven and midnight?"

Before Masters could answer, Cole touched Margo's shoulder and nodded at the man who was walking their way. "Looks like Shanks got tired of waiting."

Following Cole's gaze, Margo clamped her lips together in annoyance, then seemed to reconsider his role here. "Maybe you could steer Mr. Shanks back where he belongs and ask him the same questions?"

"Love to," Cole said, ambling away. He didn't expect a confession; he knew that questioning Shanks and Masters was basically a formality so Margo could eliminate them as potential suspects. Then again...who knew? A forty-minute drive for a thug to go wilding after the carnival closed wasn't beyond the realm of possibility.

"Hey, Blackburn!" Masters yelled, needling him from a distance. "Why is she giving the orders these days?"

Cole kept his cool, kept walking, kept his focus on short, squat Arnie of the Thirty Piercings.

"So what happened, hotshot? Where's your uniform? Where's your badge? Or aren't you a real cop anymore?"

Cole approached Shanks, smiling to hide his gut-level need to rip down a couple of tents. No, he wasn't a real cop anymore. And it cut to the core.

Twenty minutes later, Margo and Cole picked their way through the swelling crowd and, by mutual agreement, headed for the hot-foods concession. "So what do you think?" she asked, glancing up at him. "There was no pinochle game, as I suspect Shanks already told you. But supposedly, neither of them left the carnival grounds on the twentieth, or last night. Several employees said they'd seen or spoken to them after the carnival closed at eleven."

"Yeah, well," Cole returned, "the carnival's a family, and families do whatever it takes to protect their own."

Margo felt a twinge, but decided he wasn't referring to their personal situation. She sidestepped a spilled snow cone. "Sorry about Masters's mouth. I tried to shut him up. I know that had to have hurt."

"It was nothing," he said curtly. But the harsh set of his jaw belied his claim and said he didn't want to talk about it. He nodded at the big wooden menu board. "What looks good to you?"

He did, Margo thought. He always had. But that's not what he wanted to know. "I'll just have a hamburger with ketchup and relish, and a small root beer." She dug into the pouch on her belt and withdrew a five.

"Put your money away," he said, then ordered for her and added French fries for himself. "My treat."

"This isn't a date," Margo returned firmly as he pulled several bills from his wallet. "I pay my own way."

"Relax," he replied. "Just call it a thank-you for phoning the mayor and bringing me in on the case. That was worth a lot more than a burger to me."

Their food was ready in minutes. Eating while they walked, they headed for a bingo tent that seemed to double as a place to crash. They settled at one of the long tables in the back that allowed for discreet conversation.

"Okay," Cole said. "I haven't had a chance to look at the files yet, so how about telling me what happened when you interviewed the Hudson girl's roommate. You couldn't answer before when I asked if she was helpful."

Margo finished chewing, swallowed and nodded— took a sip of her root beer. "We're not sure yet, but she did tell us something that Mr. and Mrs. Hudson weren't aware of. Leanne recently broke up with someone. It didn't last long, but apparently the guy was a lot more invested in the relationship than she was."

"He threatened her?"

"No, but he was pretty upset about the breakup. The roommate—Ellie Cortino—said he phoned a lot, pressuring Leanne to give him another chance. Ellie said that when he started getting nasty, Leanne changed her cell phone number. They'd planned to have their home phone number changed, too."

"Definitely sounds like a person of interest."

"Absolutely. Ellie didn't know where he lived or how to reach him, but when she told us that Leanne met him at Flex and Burn—he's a muscle head—I got his home address from the gym and sent Brett over to his duplex. When Brett got there, the guy's SUV was gone, and there was mail in the box. We have a BOLO out on him." She took another sip of her root beer. "I doubt he had anything to do with it, though. I think he'll end up being another potential suspect that we'll cross off our list."

"Why's that?"

"Because he's new to the area, too. He was in the military and out of the country two years ago when the first murders occurred, so he wouldn't have known the particulars of the case. I'm not sure how he ended up here—he's originally from Maine—but he works at Travis Lumber now."

Cole popped a small French fry into his mouth. "If you have a BOLO out on him, I guess he didn't make it to work yesterday. Or today."

"No, he didn't. But he'd already scheduled two days off, so no one thought that was unusual."

"Could indicate premeditation."

"It could. But he'd still have to have known about the Gold Star killings to copycat the murder."

"Information like that's easy enough to find out, especially in a town the size of Charity. Everyone knows everything about everybody and they love to share it. It could've come up in conversation. Compared to the petty crimes you usually work, those murders were big." Meeting her eyes, he added succinctly, "Way too big for a rural police department to handle alone."

"Yes," Margo replied, understanding. "They were."

Cole finished the last of his fries, tucked his napkin

in the cardboard boat and rolled it into a cone. Then, as if nothing had ever changed between them, he reached for her root beer, sipped from her straw and put the cup back in front of her.

The bottom fell out of Margo's stomach.

She'd forgotten. For the past half hour they'd been partners again, all the angst and uneasiness of their past somehow miraculously shifting to the side. But with that thoughtless sip, she remembered, and suddenly she was fixated on his lips…and remembering last night's kiss.

His thoughts were still anchored in the here and now. "So," he began. "When you spoke to Bernice, did my dismissal come up?"

She could say no, but that wouldn't be honest. And whether he believed her or not, she'd always been truthful with him. "Yes. It did. But Bernice thought John and ex-Mayor Keller railroaded you. A few of the old guard are still on the town council, but Bernice said there won't be a problem." If there was, Margo thought, she'd go before council herself and fight for him.

A noisy family of seven shrieked and chatted their way to the opposite end of their table. Sharing a nod, Margo and Cole stood, gathered their paper trash and headed for one of the receptacles stationed near the tent.

"Ready to get out of here?" he asked.

"Just about. I have one more stop to make first."

The cell phone on her belt chimed. Margo checked the number in the display window, then her wristwatch. Charlie would still be on until eight when "Fish" Troutman took over; Sara would've left at five. She stepped close to the bingo tent again, away from a moving column of humanity.

"What's up, Charlie?" she said over the roar and beep of the nearby kiddie cars.

"Not a lot, but you wanted to know when the PSP had something on that blasted note you got last night."

"Any prints?" she asked, feeling a chill.

"Nope. No prints, no fibers. There were traces of powder on the masking tape and paper that were consistent with the powder from latex gloves. The star was identical to the other four. Self-adhesive, so there's not gonna be any saliva."

That was disappointing. "Okay, thanks for calling. Anything else going on?"

"Nope, not even a cat-in-a-tree call. The locals are being downright considerate tonight."

"Thank God," she said on a breath, and despite her troubles with the Lord, she meant it. "I'll be back within the hour so you can go to supper. See you then."

She closed the phone, tucked it back in its case, then filled Cole in as they resumed their walk.

"Ever wonder why he wrote the note in crayon?" Cole asked. He kept his voice low, leaning near as they ambled along. "Or why he signs his work with gold stars? Like the sticky stars elementary-school teachers put on little kids' papers."

"Yes, and I made the same connection you did. School days. But did he do it to throw us off or is it real? As for printing the note in crayon, that could've been done to disguise his handwriting."

"It could," Cole said. "But it could also mean something to him. When we investigated the original murders, we thought the killer was marking the victims with gold stars so the media would give him some cool name like the Zodiac or Son of Sam. Now that he's using crayons, I think we should look at it differently." He backtracked suddenly, seeming to remember he was only a consultant. "I mean, *you* might want to look at it differently."

Margo chewed her lip. "You're right. If the crayons are important to him, we didn't have enough information last time. We need to look at teachers. Past and present."

"Students, too."

Margo paused for a second, then continued walking. "The Hudson girl didn't go to school here, though. She and her parents only moved here a year ago when her dad retired from the military."

Cole grunted an assent, then went on. "Let me do some digging anyway. I remember a few of the teachers and some of the kids who got my attention in one way or another when I worked here. But I have a feeling this guy keeps a low profile—isn't a seasoned troublemaker."

"Why?"

"I'm not sure. It's just a hunch." He glanced down at her. "School doesn't open for a week, but the secretaries should be in. If the library's open, they might have a few old yearbooks we can look at. Maybe something will jump out at us."

"Like what?"

Margo felt a jittery run of attraction when he tipped his head closer to hers.

"Seeing what clubs, sports and activities the first two girls were involved in might be helpful. It's possible they had something in common with the Hudson girl besides blond hair."

Margo gave herself a mental shake—made herself focus. "*If* the crayons and stars mean something to the killer, and *if* the killer is or was a teacher or student here. With Leanne Hudson growing up elsewhere, I'm skeptical."

Up ahead, the Ferris wheel came to a stop. So did Margo's heart.

And for one poignant moment, she and Cole paused

to watch the couple at the very top of the ride. They watched them laugh…watched them rock to and fro… watched them kiss. Cole's eyes met hers and held for a second, then their uneasy gazes darted away.

Margo set her feet in motion again. "Anyway," she said after taking a breath, "there's still a chance that the note isn't related to the murders. It could've come from someone who simply enjoys stirring the pot."

"The star was identical to those on the Hudson girl," Cole reminded her.

"And they're for sale at thousands of department and stationery stores across the country."

A couple pushing an umbrella stroller cut across in front of them. "It's just so frustrating," Margo went on. "I know I'll see the Hudsons tomorrow at the funeral, and they'll want to hear that we're making progress. I wish I knew what to say to them."

Cole took her hand, then squeezed and released it. "You'll find the right words, just as you did with Adam this afternoon. You know how to make people feel better. It's your gift."

There it was again: that big, unwelcome lump rising like a hen's egg in her throat, making it difficult to talk. "Thank you. I hope you're right." She halted then. They'd reached their destination.

For a moment, Cole seemed to wonder why they'd stopped. Then a slow smile warmed his rugged features and he started to chuckle, delight shining in his brown eyes.

"Come on, don't play games," she said. "You knew where we were going."

"No, I really didn't," he said, still laughing. "Especially since I was lying through my teeth earlier, and you knew it." His smile softened. "I just…I just didn't want you messing with those guys on your own. And know what? I shouldn't have worried. You were strong. You were great."

Dear God. If he didn't stop being so nice to her, he would see just exactly how strong she wasn't. "Obviously," she replied airily, "that's because I learned from the best."

Margo produced the five-dollar bill he'd refused earlier, put it in his hand and folded his fingers around it. "Now enjoy. Your candy apple's on me."

FIVE

Margo hurried into the diner the next morning, knowing she'd be rushing to catch up all day. Instead of Snooze, she'd hit the off button on her alarm clock when it rang at six, and had fallen back to sleep until six thirty-five. She'd broken all records showering and dressing.

Pert little Mitzi Abbott scooted to Margo's end of the lunch counter, her white sneakers squeaking on the black-and-white floor tiles. As always, she wore a smile that made half the boys in town crazy, and a pink uniform dress that could've come straight from the set of Mel's Diner.

"Hey, Margo. What can I get for you?"

"Black coffee and an apple Danish to go," Margo said, smiling back and dropping to one of the round black-and-chrome stools. "Don't heat it, though. I'm running late." She rested her forearms on the cherry-red counter and tried to arrange her thoughts over the wake-up-and-start-your-day music flowing from a speaker somewhere. Her mother had phoned the station last night while she was covering for Charlie. But as she was assuring her mom that she was being careful, a call came in from a frightened sixteen-year-old who was home alone and feared that a man in a gray SUV was watching her house. She'd called Charlie at the diner and driven out to the Trask place. The man in question had simply been looking for an address, but the girl had worried because she had long blond hair.

People were getting increasingly nervous. Two years ago, there'd been five days between the murders. Now, according to the girl, people she knew weren't just staying away from the park. They were counting down the days, watching their calendars.

Mitzi strode over with a foam cup and Danish in a to-go box, then directed Margo's attention to a ruggedly attractive man sitting in one of the back booths. He wore a burgundy polo shirt and faded jeans.

"Looks like you have an admirer," she said, grinning. "He's been checking you out over his newspaper since you came in."

Margo hid a tingle of excitement and paid her bill. "He's not an admirer," she said, accepting her change, then leaving a dollar for Mitzi. "He used to be my fiancé."

Slipping the rest of her change into her pocket, she walked back to Cole's booth. "Isn't Jenna feeding you this morning?"

Cole set aside the morning paper. "She offered, but I don't have the time to do her Belgian waffles justice. I just came in to scan the headlines and grab a quick cup of coffee. Sherry from the office called last night. I have to drive back this morning to meet with my new client." He spoke drily as he stood, tossed a few bills on the table and grabbed the newspaper. "Apparently, there's no shortage of wives who doubt their husbands these days."

His statement shouldn't have given her a lift, but it did. Margo walked with him as he dropped the newspaper in the wooden wall caddy and continued toward the door. "Not your kind of work?"

"Let's just say I prefer bringing families together, not ripping them apart. I had a missing-persons gig last month. That was feel-good stuff."

He opened the door for her, then followed her into the morning sun and milky-blue sky. Digging his keys out of his jeans, he moved toward his truck parked in the side lot. "Well, I'm out of here."

Margo nodded. "Me, too. Have a safe trip."

"Thanks. And if anything comes up—"

"I'll call your cell phone."

"Good. See you." He started across the lot, then halted, turned around and smiled. "Hey. Thanks for the candy apple last night."

"Thanks for the burger," she replied. Then trying to ignore another pang of disappointment, she crossed the street to the stone-and-timber police station. She had to stop feeling hurt every time he said goodbye.

He would always be leaving.

The funeral was as heartrending as the Morgan and Kennicott services had been. After the family and friends had exited the white nondenominational church at the end of Sassafras Street and started the slow drive to Leanne Hudson's final resting place, Margo returned to the station and threw herself into work. She'd hoped that being in church again, praying and singing along with the congregation, would somehow renew her faith in a loving God. She missed that feeling of contentment and rightness. But all she could think of as the organ played and people filed out, wiping their eyes, was the terrible, unnecessary reason for the service. And that separateness claimed her again.

She was surprised to bump into Reverend Landers late that day as she was taking a half gallon of milk from the Quick Stop's dairy case. Her shift was over, and she was looking forward to another shower. The heat and humidity were high again today, with no rain in sight, though forecasters kept saying it was on the way.

"Hello, Margo," the graying cleric said, smiling and extending his hand to shake hers.

He was a few inches taller than Margo's five feet six, a good eighty pounds heavier and thirty years older. His black jacket and white collar were gone, replaced by a light blue plaid cotton shirt over his gray trousers. Silver-framed glasses brought out the kind sparkle in his pale blue eyes. "It was good to see you in church today."

Margo smiled back. Paul Landers was a good man, but he'd never been one to waste time on pleasantries when there were souls to be saved. "I needed to be there for the Hudson family," she said.

"Still mad at God?"

Why shade the truth? He knew how she felt. "I am, and I'm sorry to say, the reasons for that keep multiplying."

"Oh?" He tipped his head, encouraging her to go on, but Margo suspected he understood.

"You saw all those tears today."

"I did, indeed," he said, his compassion showing. "That was one of the saddest services I've ever led. But you're blaming the wrong guy. God didn't hurt the Hudson girl. Man with his gift of free will did. Jesus came to teach us the way to live, but not everyone got the message."

That was an understatement if she ever heard one, Margo thought. She smiled and nodded as a woman she couldn't immediately place passed by with her arms full of purchases and waved a few fingers.

"Should've grabbed a basket," she called over her shoulder. "Tell your mom to call me when she gets back."

Yes, she would certainly do that if she could remember the woman's name. It came to her. Shirley Fredrick.

"You know," Landers said when Margo gave him her attention again. "You'll have to forgive Him sooner or later. Otherwise, you're only hurting yourself."

"I know that," she returned. "But unconditional love shouldn't always be a one-way street. Every so often, it would be nice if He answered a few prayers—if He gave something back."

Landers seemed to consider that. He didn't remind her that she'd been blessed with good health and a quick mind, a job that provided her with creature comforts and a half-dozen other things. He knew what she meant because he knew what she'd lost.

"What do you want from Him, Margo?"

"It's a long list," she said quietly. "But helping me find a killer would be a good start."

"Well, then, you know what to do."

No, she didn't. If she knew, she'd do it. "What?"

Landers smiled. "What do you do when a friend you care deeply about continues to disappoint you? Do you write her off? Do you tell him to take a hike?" Landers opened the dairy cooler and pulled out a carton of heavy cream, then touched her arm. "Talk to Him."

Twenty minutes later, after dropping off her milk—no point giving Him a chance to curdle it—and changing to black shorts and a sleeveless white knit with a scalloped neckline and tiny black buttons, Margo drove her red Grand Cherokee two miles outside of town. She turned off the highway onto a tarred and chipped secondary road that cut through a heavily forested area. Presently, she pulled into a long, shaded rock-and-dirt driveway overrun with weeds.

Shutting off the Cherokee's engine, she stared through the windshield at the unfinished one-story house with the high-peaked roof—a house that would never be her home. There was no cedar siding on it yet, no ornamental stone. Just white, vapor-barrier "home wrap" over the plywood walls. The thermal-paned windows still bore the manufacturer's stickers. But the covered porch and lovely front door of wood-toned steel and stained glass said the house held real promise.

Sadly, the red-and-white For Sale sign hanging from a Realtor's post took that promise away.

Leaving her car, she walked to the house and the dense mixed forest that surrounded it. There were maples, wild cherry, pines and hemlocks, and hardy beech that kept squirrels and chipmunks happily stuffing their pouches. Close to the house where the trees had been cleared, ferns clustered around a few fallen timbers.

Margo climbed the steps and sat on the porch floor, too many what-might've-beens going through her mind.

She'd loved coming here. With help from a friend who owned a construction company, Cole had framed and roofed the house. Another friend had helped him do the rough wiring and plumbing. It seemed there was nothing the man couldn't do when he set his mind to it...except believe her.

Overhead, a patch of blue sky and tattered white clouds peered through the leafy treetops.

"Okay," she said, quietly addressing the Heavens. "Let's talk." She'd always felt closer to God here in this natural cathedral than she ever had in a church. "I'm still mad. But you know that. You know everything that's going on." She raised her voice. "So why aren't you doing anything about it?"

Halting, not liking the sound of her anger in this special place, she dropped her voice again. "I'm sure there's a reason for all the heartache I've witnessed lately, but what is it? What good did it do to deprive this world of a bright young woman who wanted to become a doctor? Leanne Hudson could've alleviated so much suffering—done so much good. And yet you let a killer end her life and the lives of two other girls, and did nothing. Now their families are looking to me for solutions."

She swallowed, feeling the tears come. "And by the way, where were you when I prayed for help when my relationship with Cole went south? Not to mention the prayers I said asking you to spare my father after his stroke. I did my best. I gave you my devotion. I dedicated my life to helping others. But when I came to you and asked for your grace, you said no." Her tears were rolling now and she let them run.

"Take a look around you," she said, feeling her anger rise again. "See this house? This was supposed to be my reward for living a good life. I was supposed to have a home and a loving husband and maybe a couple of babies. But again," she added, "you said no. Forgive me, but it's hard to keep believing in a caring God when I give, give, give, and you take, take, take."

Wiping her tears, she stood, then slowly strolled across the porch to the bay window. She peered inside at the space that would've been their great room, saw the soaring cathedral ceiling, the brown paper stapled between the wall studs, and knew there was fuzzy pink fiberglass behind it. She and Cole had insulated all the rooms together, assuring that their home would stay warm and cozy in the winters ahead. Afterward, with lights from a

generator, and a space heater to chase the chill of those
early-spring nights, they'd sat on the dusty subfloor and
eased their backs against a wall. And they'd sipped hot
cocoa from a thermos, dreaming of the day they'd move
in.

A gust of wind picked up the cooler air in the woods,
raising gooseflesh on Margo's bare arms and legs.
Another gust ruffled the pines at the side of the house.
She looked up at the clouds moving across the sky, thinking that maybe the weatherman was right after all. Maybe
rain was on the way.

That's when she saw the first tinges of orange edging
a few maple leaves and sighed. In a matter of weeks, September would give way to October, and October would
move inexorably on to winter's howling winds, snow and
ice. She swallowed hard.

Pennsylvania winters could be harsh without hot
cocoa and dreams.

The sound of a vehicle approaching jerked her attention from the trees, and Margo felt a quick jolt of adrenaline. A black Silverado had turned off the secondary road
and was coming up the driveway.

Chills raced the length of her. Was that an answer?
Was God sending Cole back to her? Or was his arrival
just a coincidence?

Turning away, she wiped her face again, then cleared
her throat and descended the steps to meet him.

He got out of his truck, looking as surprised to see
her as she was to see him. "Hello," he said tentatively,
chinking his keys in his hand as he approached. He was
looking at her strangely. And the closer he got, the more
concern showed on his features.

Dear God, Margo thought, trying not to cringe.
Please. I know I was disrespectful. But if You never do

another thing for me in my life, don't let him see that I've been crying. She was sure the next words out of Cole's mouth would be, "What are you doing here, and why are your eyes red?"

They weren't.

"Have you been inside?" he asked, his expression betraying nothing.

"No, I...just took a peek through the window."

"You could've gone in." He looked toward a stack of rocks piled at the west corner of the foundation. "The spare key's still under the rock with all the fossils on it. Did you look for it?"

And still he didn't ask what brought her here. "No, I couldn't do that. This is your house." Folding her arms, Margo studied the scrub grass in the driveway. "I was told you'd had a few bids on the house. I was surprised to see that the Realtor's sign is still up."

She glanced up at him, but he looked away, his voice gruff. "The bids weren't high enough. I put a lot of work into this house. I can't see giving it away."

"No," she replied. "You shouldn't. I just thought with the housing market not doing well right now, you would've jumped at the chance to sell."

"Nope." Taking a few steps back to his truck, he grabbed a broom and dustpan from the bed, then selected a key from his ring and nodded for her to precede him up the steps to the porch. "As long as you're here, you might as well come inside while I take a walk-through. I check the place out from time to time. You know, make sure it hasn't been vandalized or the squirrels haven't moved in." He nodded at the broom and dustpan. "I left a mess last night. I'll just clean it up, then check the door and window locks."

He was here last night after the carnival? And he came

back periodically to check the house? She hadn't known that. Then again, he didn't have to go through town to get here from Pittsburgh. It would be easy to keep his comings and goings private. In fact, she thought, finally paying attention to the pale blue dress shirt he wore open-throated with his dark jeans and boots, he was probably just returning from his meeting at Sharp.

For an instant she wanted to ask how often he'd done one of his walk-throughs—then decided it was best not to know how many times he'd been here and chosen not to see her.

Cole opened the house and ushered her inside. Tamping down a flood of nostalgia, Margo followed him through the great room with its vaulted ceiling to a hall with three bedrooms and a home office. The mess he referred to was in the smallest room. A saber saw lay on the dusty plywood floor below a set of sawbucks, surrounded by chunks of Sheetrock and crumpled paper. The office had walls now.

"You're working in here again," she said, not sure why, though some hopeful part of her wondered if he'd changed his mind about selling.

"Seemed like a good idea. The Sheetrock was already stacked in the back bedroom. I figured that doing a little more work might help to sell the house. I don't like seeing it sitting empty like this."

She didn't, either. It looked lonely and unloved out here in the dark woods. It would hurt to see someone else living in it.

Cole set the broom and dustpan aside, then crossed to the corner of the room to pull the wastebasket closer before tossing paper and Sheetrock into it. Margo picked up the broom and went to work.

"You don't have to do that," he said.

"You're helping me with the case. I can do a little something for you." It felt strange, but right, to be cleaning up in here. Probably because, for a few minutes at least, she could pretend it was still her house, too.

"I would've swept up last night after the carnival, but I figured since I'd be around for a while anyway, there was no hurry." He waited for Margo to sweep the dust and small pieces into a pile, then crouched on the floor to hold the dustpan.

When he spoke again, there was a forced casualness in his voice. "That was kind of fun last night at the carnival, all things considered."

"Yes, it was. All things considered." Margo felt a rush of nerves as she finished sweeping the dust onto the pan, then continued hesitantly. "It brought back a few memories."

He rose, nodded and emptied the dustpan. A tiny smile touched his lips. "You were afraid of the Ferris wheel that night."

Margo smiled back, her heart swelling with the memory of *that night*. "And you made stupid chicken noises until I agreed to ride with you."

His smile grew. "You didn't say they were stupid then."

Margo stood the broom up in the corner. "Well, that night I was more interested in the way you looked than the way you sounded."

"Oh? How did I look?"

She met his eyes. The same way he looked right now—too tall, too well built and too good. But she felt vulnerable enough right now and couldn't say it. "I guess you looked…okay."

He chuckled, a gentleness entering his dark eyes. "You looked okay that night, too."

They stood there for a moment, letting the three-year-old memory take them back to Charity's Fourth of July Fireman's Celebration. Cole had been in town visiting an old college roommate and his girlfriend, who coincidentally worked for Margo's dad in his accounting office. There'd been an instant spark when Allison and Mark had introduced them, as well as an immediate connection, with both of them working in law enforcement. She'd balked when he'd insisted that she ride the Ferris wheel with him. She was a cop, he'd teased, and she *had* to have more starch than she was showing him. *"Just hold on to me and you'll be safe."*

Their kiss at the top of the wheel had been magic. Margo had fallen hard for him that night, and the feeling had been mutual. Soon afterward, Cole left Manhattan and joined the Charity police force.

"Well," Cole said softly when the moment seemed to last a little too long. "I'll just make sure everything's locked up before we leave." He glanced through the doorway to the hall. "Maybe you can check the living room and kitchen while I do the bedrooms?"

"Sure," she replied, feeling a lovely lift in her heart. "I'll see you on the porch." She was afraid to think that frail bridge between them had strengthened a little today, yet she couldn't control the hopeful part of her that insisted it was true.

Smiling, she checked the window locks in the living room, then wandered into the bare-bones kitchen and did the same. It was three times the size of her kitchen at home, and she found herself visualizing appliances and cabinets...a table in the cozy breakfast nook. She peered out the window at the partially cleared "backyard." One night as they'd looked through this window together, she'd told Cole it was a yard made for a barbecue pit, half a dozen bird feeders and a great big swing and slide set for their kids. He'd laughed and kissed her then.

"How many kids?"

"Let's start with two and see what happens."

He'd chuckled. *"Sounds doable. Let's make that our first order of business as soon as we're married."*

"I love you so much," she'd said, softening her voice.

"Guess what?" he'd returned warmly. *"I love you, too."*

Margo's cell phone chimed out a melody, jolting her back to the present. She pulled it from her pocket—then felt a slight letdown when she saw her mother's cell phone number in the ID window. She'd promised to call her back last night, and forgotten.

Cole stepped into the kitchen just as she raised the phone to her ear and said, "Hi, Mom."

Her spirits dipped lower when he froze, then motioned to the doorless opening leading to the basement, indicating that that part of the house needed to be checked, too. Nodding that she understood, she waited until he'd descended the stairs, then spoke to her mother again. Would there *ever* come a day when her timing wasn't off?

"Sorry I didn't get back to you last night. By the time I returned to the office, it was too late to call."

"Thank you for being considerate, honey, but after hearing you say you were going out on a stalker call, I would've preferred to know that you were all right." Her mom had a sweet, melodic voice. Margo's dad used to say it was half Dorothy Gale, half munchkin. "I'm fine. The stalker turned out to be a guy looking for an address. The girl overreacted."

"I can see why, considering what happened. Honey, would you like me to come home? I know I can't help with the police work, but I could do some laundry for you—see that you get a decent meal once in a while."

"No, Mom, I'm good. Just stay with Miriam for a few more days and enjoy yourself. But keep in touch. If I'm not home when you call, just leave a message on my machine."

"I will, but you have to remember to pick it up. I left a message last night. Did you get it?"

No, she hadn't. She hadn't picked up any of her messages in the past two days. "Whoops."

"Honey, there's no point in having a machine if you're not going to use it."

"I know. It's just been crazy around here, and when I get home at night, the only thing I want to do is crash."

"Margo, are you getting enough sleep?"

"I'm trying." There was no point in telling her that it's hard to sleep with Cole back in town and a killer on the loose. A killer who'd recently become her pen pal.

"Try harder," her mother said softly. "I love you and I want you to stay healthy. What time is it there?"

Margo smiled. "Twenty minutes to eight. The same time it is in North Carolina."

"Okay, smarty pants," she returned, laughing. "Go to bed. Get some sleep. Where are you?"

She'd been waiting for that question. Margo stared at the basement doorway and hoped he wouldn't be wearing that closed look when he came back upstairs.

"I'm with Cole, Mom."

SIX

Cole stepped onto the porch, locked the front door, then paused to study Margo as she stood staring out at the rain. She looked uneasy, and it didn't take a mind reader to know why. But despite what she thought, he didn't blame Charlotte for trying to keep her close after Frank died. He did blame her for making Margo think she had to cancel her own plans. Her own life.

Not that he would've had a big part in it.

Shoving his keys into the pocket of his Levi's, he walked to where she stood under the porch roof. "Is your mom doing okay?"

Margo turned to him, apology in her green eyes. "Yes, she's fine. She's just worried about me."

That startled him. "You told her about the note?"

"No. I wouldn't do that. But the latest murder has her on edge. She was afraid I still take the shortcut through Woodland Park when I run at night."

Cole didn't breathe for a second or two. "Do you?"

"No." She hesitated for a few seconds. "She sends you her best."

Her best? He could've used some of that eleven months ago. There would have been no need to cancel the caterer, the hall, the sound system, or disappoint diner-owner

Aggie Benson, who also owned the local flower shop. Good old Aggie, who'd told him she was more upset about their broken engagement than she was of losing a sale.

"You're still angry," Margo said when he didn't immediately reply. "You still blame her."

Cole moved closer, eased against the porch railing. Then he, too, looked out at the rain because it bothered him to look into those sad eyes. It was falling in big drops, splotching the roofs of their vehicles. "To be honest, I was more ticked off with your dad for leaving her out of the loop when it came to finances or anything else that didn't apply to homemaking."

"That was his way. He adored her. She was content to leave business matters to him, and he let her be the homemaker she wanted to be." She reached out to touch his arm, then seemed to think better of it and withdrew her hand. "But you're not being honest when you say you weren't angry. I saw the look on your face when you realized I was talking to her. The walls went up. You shut down."

Maybe he had, but… "Angry's the wrong word."

"What's the right one?"

Pushing away from the railing, he wandered to the top of the steps leading down to the driveway. "I don't know. Frustrated? Aggravated? Discouraged? All of them?" He turned back to her. "But that's ancient history, so let's not rehash it. I'm glad she's doing well."

He saw it in her eyes. Now *she* was frustrated. She *wanted* to rehash it. But he wasn't interested in trotting his pride out like a sacrificial lamb to the slaughter again. Once was more than enough.

Margo averted her gaze again. "She flew to North Carolina a few days ago to visit an old friend who's also lost her husband. Miriam was her maid of honor. They stayed close after the Hollands moved to Durham." She paused for a beat. "I'm really proud of her. It's the first time she's flown anywhere without my dad."

Despite his reluctance to discuss the past, Margo's statement begged a question. "She's handling things better now?"

"She has a fair grasp of her finances, but when she needs help, she calls one of the advisors at Dad's old office."

"She doesn't call you?"

Her slender throat worked as she swallowed. "No. She still cries sometimes because she misses my dad so much, but…well, you know how devoted they were." She turned from the rain to meet his eyes, her voice almost challenging now. "After thirty-six years with him, she's entitled to cry when she needs to."

Cole nodded. He'd never disputed that. It was Charlotte's overwhelming need that got him. But that was better left unsaid. "When you speak to her again, give her my best, too."

When she sent him a disbelieving stare, he went on. "That wasn't lip service. I don't dislike your mother. She's a good woman." She just hadn't done right by her daughter or by him.

Suddenly the memories started getting to him, and his chest tightened. He needed to wrap this up. "The bottom line is, things happen for a reason, and there's no going back."

It wasn't his intention, but somehow he'd opened the door to the discussion he didn't want to have.

"What was our reason?" she asked quietly.

He couldn't say the words. Besides, she'd heard them before. "I don't know. Maybe we wouldn't have been happy together. Maybe we wouldn't have made it in the long run."

"No," she replied firmly. "That wasn't our reason. At least it's not the reason you believe. But we're not going to talk about that, are we?"

Before he could say, "No, we aren't, because there's no point," she walked to the top step.

"I need to get back to town. I told Jenna I'd stop by the Blackberry for a few minutes, and I don't want to keep her up too late."

He didn't want her to leave. It made no sense, but even with her voice crisp and her hackles up, he wanted her to stay. "Wait until the rain stops."

She shook her head. "No, I think it's only going to get worse. I'd better go now."

"You're right," he agreed, hiding his disappointment. "I should go, too." He knew what she'd meant. It was best that they stop before they waded into deeper waters and their tentative…friendship? working relationship?… went down like the *Titanic*. For both of their sakes, they needed to ignore the past, and focus on catching a killer.

Lightning crashed, and thunder rumbled as the rain pounded down in a flashing storm straight out of the Old Testament. Jenna stepped through the squealing screen door leading to her pretty porch, wincing at the sound. "One of these days, I'm going to remember to oil those hinges. It sounds like a banshee's wail."

She put a tray down on the porch's glass-topped white wicker table. "Margo, are you sure you don't want to talk inside? I know we really need the rain, but this is a bit much."

Yes, she was sure. Cole was inside, and she didn't want

him to overhear them if he happened to come downstairs. "Afraid of a little lightning?" she teased.

"Not me. I'm fine with it. I was thinking of you."

"A week's worth of ninety-degree heat and humidity tends to make people edgy, so I'm delighted to see the rain."

Jenna assessed her curiously. She wore purple capris with a boatneck purple-and-white knit top. Tonight, her sun-streaked, dark blond hair was pulled back in a ponytail. "Who's edgy? Anyone I know?"

"Me. I need to cool down."

Grinning, Jenna segued to another subject. "Speaking of cooling down, when I was shopping for groceries yesterday, I overheard two women talking in one of the aisles. Regardless of the heat, apparently people have been staying away from the community pool at Woodland Park."

"I heard that, too. And it doesn't make any sense, particularly since the pool closes before dark. But some fears aren't logical."

With another glance at the deluge, Jenna poured iced tea from a long, clear pitcher into their frosty glasses, added slices of lemon to the rims and garnished their drinks with a sprig of fresh mint.

Margo smiled. "You didn't have to get fancy. I would've been happy with tap water in a jelly jar."

"Don't be silly. I do it for my guests. You're *at least* that important to me." She took a seat beside Margo on the padded wicker sofa. "So what's going on? When you and Cole came in, you both looked tense. Or should I say edgy? What is it? The case or him?"

Margo picked up her tea and looked out at the rain. "Tonight, it's him. Boy, is it him."

"I thought as much." Taking a spoon from the tray,

Jenna added sugar to her tea and stirred. Ice cubes tinkled against her glass. "You had an argument."

"No. No, an argument would've been a good thing. We would've said what needed to be said, not danced around the issue." She sipped at her tea, then realized that as refreshing as it was, her stomach wasn't ready for it. Returning it to the table, she lowered her voice. "I never told you about the breakup."

"You told me some of it. I know John Wilcox dismissed Cole for insubordination. And I know that when your dad died, you postponed your wedding to be with your mother."

"Her heart was in shreds. I didn't think she'd ever stop crying." She shifted on the floral cushion to face Jenna. "She needed me. You know what it's like, being an only child. Your mother needed you, too, when your dad passed away."

"Yes, but they're very different women. My mom was outgoing—still is. She bowls, she takes tai chi classes. She even worked in retail for a time. Your mom's whole world was you and your dad."

Margo couldn't sit any longer. Getting up, she walked to the railing. Cool mist from the rain hit her face and arms as the thunder continued to roll and lightning flashed again.

"I want to tell you about this. But when I'm finished, I'd like to ask you a question, and I'd really appreciate an honest answer."

"Then that's what you'll get. Shoot."

Margo didn't need to gather her thoughts. Except for the murder, she'd thought of little else since Cole showed up two days ago. "When Cole lost his job, he wanted me to quit the department, too. But we were getting married, and he was building our house, and I said no. We needed an income. Thanks to John blackballing him, he couldn't find another job in the area. It nearly killed him, Jenna. He was born to be a cop. He was working in one of the Manhattan precincts when we met."

"Okay. Go on."

"When he couldn't find police work in the area, he contacted his precinct captain."

"Let me guess," Jenna said. "His captain said to come back. And you said no."

"Yes." The wind shifted, blowing rain to the edge of the porch now, and Margo moved away from the white wood railing. "We wanted kids, and I didn't want to raise them in a city. So," she went on, "he finally took the P.I. job, just to *have* a job. Problem was, by that time we were arguing so much, when he asked me to move up our wedding and live in a Pittsburgh suburb, I was so afraid of being uprooted and jobless if the marriage failed…"

"You said no again."

"Yeah. But the big no came after my dad died. Cole was great about our postponing the wedding until my mom was stronger. But when months passed, he pushed for an elopement. He said he was tired of living alone, tired of putting off the family and home that he wanted, and I was blind if I couldn't see that my mother was never going to get better until I backed off and let her stand on her own two feet. He said she was manipulating the situation so she wouldn't lose me, too."

That utterly bereft feeling settled in Margo's chest. "My mom was a mess, he was angry and unhappy, and I was the key to both of them being whole. I couldn't take it, Jenna. I loved him, but I was keeping him from the life he wanted and needed. I gave back the ring, and he…he accepted it."

Tears stung her eyes again, but she refused to cry. It was time to toughen up. "He made it pretty clear that I wasn't important enough to wait for. He wanted to get on with his life. So I let him."

Jenna's brow furrowed. "Is that what he said?"

"No, he said that taking care of my mom was just one more excuse in a long line of excuses. He said I should've told him months ago that I wanted out and saved us both some time."

Now she needed the iced tea. She went to Jenna's wicker grouping and took her glass from the table. Sipped. Swallowed. A boulder would've gone down more easily. "I told him I loved him more than he could ever know. He called me a liar."

Jenna put Margo's drink back on the table and wrapped her in a gentle hug. "I'm so sorry," she murmured. "How are the two of you handling working together?"

Stepping back, Margo released an unsteady breath. "I can't speak for him, but I'm walking on eggshells most of the time. Tonight I wanted to clear the air, but he shut me down. No surprise there. He's got a lot of pride. He refuses to talk about anything that might put a little chink in his armor. Last night someone gave him a bad time about not being a cop anymore. When I sympathized, he said it was nothing and changed the subject. But I know *him,* so I know how much it hurt."

Margo walked around, crossed her arms, felt the cooler wind on her bare legs and realized she should've changed clothes instead of driving straight here from the house. "So? Was I at fault? Am I the reason we're not together anymore?"

When Jenna sighed, Margo knew she wouldn't like her answer.

"I think there's plenty of blame to go around," she said

kindly. "There could've been more understanding on his part, but there could've also been more give on yours." She paused. "The other thing is, you said something that seemed significant to me."

"What?"

"You said that when he asked you to move to Pittsburgh, you were arguing so much you were afraid of being uprooted and jobless *if the marriage failed*."

"Yes?"

Jenna looked at her pointedly, trying to make her see the importance in those last few words. Then, she did. Margo drew a breath, her thoughts suddenly racing. Was it possible that the moment she'd decided to stay in Charity in case the marriage failed, she'd already given up on it?

"I'm sorry," Jenna said. "It was something that jumped out at me when you—"

She stopped abruptly as someone knocked on that squeaky screen door to announce his presence, then opened it. Someone with a warm, deep voice.

Margo felt her knees go weak as Cole stepped onto the porch. "Sorry for the interruption," he said, then wiggled the door back and forth. "Want me to oil these hinges for you, Jenna?"

Praying that the sound of the rain had drowned out their voices, Margo watched Jenna flash a warm smile and answer smoothly. "I can do it, thanks. I'm pretty handy with a can of WD-40."

When he grinned back and closed the door, she said, "So what's up? Do you need more towels? Coffee? A snack before lights-out?"

"No, but thanks. You run a tight ship. I haven't needed anything that wasn't already provided since I got here." His gaze shifted to Margo. "I noticed that your car was still in the driveway when I got out of the shower. I just wanted to tell you that I got the green light to check out the elementary and high school's yearbooks, so I'll do that on Monday morning."

"Sounds good," she said, silently applauding herself for her even delivery.

"But," he continued, "the library's open on Saturday, and they have yearbooks, too. Not all, but a few. I thought I'd stop there in the morning before I head back home. I have a dinner tomorrow night."

Margo stilled. He had a dinner tomorrow night? Was it business or pleasure? An obligation…or a date?

The tiny voice at the back of her mind was only too happy to answer: his life didn't stop when he signed on to help you. He doesn't live here anymore. He has friends and interests somewhere else now.

"Anyway, if you're free—"

"For…dinner?" she asked before she stopped to think. When he sent her a blank stare, she knew she'd made an embarrassing misstep.

"No, to meet me at the library at nine tomorrow morning."

Hoping she didn't look as foolish as she felt, she said, "No, I can't. I have phone calls to return and a pile of paperwork to do. You go ahead. I hope you find something helpful."

"I do, too." He sent Jenna an apologetic grin. "I'll get out of your hair here in just a second." He met Margo's eyes again. "I was looking at the list of community events Jenna leaves in the rooms. There's a church picnic on Sunday after services. If I get back in time, I might go. To services, anyway."

Jenna looked at the two of them, then smiled and made an excuse to leave. "Pardon me for a minute? I have to check on something in the dining room. Margo, I'll see you inside."

"Okay, I'll be there in a few minutes." She waited until Jenna had disappeared behind the screen door before she replied. "I didn't know about the picnic. Other than the funeral service, I haven't been to church in a while." She paused. "I'm surprised that you still go. It wasn't high on your priority list when we were together."

"Yeah, I know. But when things got messed up... Well, I thought I'd give God a shot. I wasn't doing so hot on my own." With a wry twist of his lips, he shrugged. "Well, maybe I'll see you on Sunday."

She wasn't sure about that. "Maybe. Have a nice time at your dinner."

"Thanks," he said. "I plan to."

But that didn't answer any of the questions banging around in her head, did it?

Rain dripped off her hair as Margo unlocked the side door to her house ten minutes later and rushed inside the kitchen. Despite the storm's ferocity her attention was still on Cole—and hating the very idea that he might be dating. Kicking off her wet sneakers, she locked the door behind her, then grabbed a few paper towels from the dispenser on the countertop to dry her face and arms.

There's nothing you can do about it, that intrusive little voice preached. *You heard Jenna. You're not completely blameless in all of this. Did you give up on the engagement even before your dad died and your mom needed help? You never did answer.*

No, she hadn't.

Deeply troubled, she changed to yellow seersucker pajamas, then looked deeply into her memories—tried to see past the hurt in her heart for the truth. It took a while, but she found it. Returning to the kitchen, she poured a glass of orange juice and headed for the tiny office off her living room.

No, she had not given up on her love for him. Yes, she'd been frustrated with the tension and their numerous arguments, but she honestly had wanted to wait until Cole was happy with P.I. work before she moved. The good times before the bad times had been too wonderful to ignore—and somewhere in her heart, she knew times could be good again. She'd wanted his new position to work out. But job or no job, house or no house…she truly would've moved.

The red light was blinking on her answering machine when she entered the office. Margo turned on the desk lamp and pressed the play button, then listened as she sat down and turned on her computer.

The first message was from the mayor saying that the town council wanted to install parking meters on their streets. Bernice thought Margo should attend the next council meeting and share her opinion. That was easy. None of the merchants wanted their customers "penalized" for shopping in their stores. When street parking filled up, people could park in the municipal parking lot and pay the piper. She wasn't sure how much revenue the parking meters there provided, but to Margo's way of thinking, it was enough.

The second message was from her mother, and contained basically the same words she'd heard from her this evening: don't take the shortcut through Woodland Park when you run at night.

The third message made her vault from her chair to stand over the machine and listen. The hollow voice seemed to come from the bottom of a well. Was he only disguising his voice or using a voice synthesizer?

"You know who this is, don't you?"

Margo's heart beat fast. Yes, she did. Quickly, she checked the caller ID history on her phone. Goose bumps ran the length of her when she saw the vaguely familiar cell phone number.

Him again—one more line before he hung up: "I really wanted to go out tonight, but it's raining too hard. I'd catch my...death."

Margo started to call the station, then abruptly hung up and phoned Cole at Jenna's B&B.

"Did you change your mind about the library?" he asked when he picked up.

"No. Do you have your copy of the Gold Star files with you right now?"

"No, they're in my valise, locked in my truck. I decided to skip the library and get going first thing in the morning. What's up? You sound nervous."

"Not nervous, surprised. I just retrieved the messages from my answering machine. I got a call. From him."

Tension seemed to crackle over the phone line. "I'll be there in a minute."

"No, wait. I was going to have Fish check out something in Leanne Hudson's file, but he's new, and I need it fast. I'll drive downtown and check myself."

"The files are barely fifty feet away. I'll get them. What do you need?"

"Leanne's cell phone number. It should be in Brett's notes. We got it from Ellie Cortino when we questioned her the other day. The phone wasn't among Hudson's effects, but Ellie said she was always leaving it somewhere, so no one thought that was unusual. I think our killer has it."

"If he does, it can be tracked. *He* can be tracked."

"That's what I'm counting on." A beep sounded in her earpiece just as Cole said something.

"Cole, I'm getting a call from Fish."

"Okay, I'll see you in a few minutes."

Margo pushed the flash button on her phone. "Fish? What is it?"

"An accident out by the Hawkins Run Bridge. Old Elmer Fox ran his truck off the road and into a bank. An out-of-stater called it in. Paramedics and a tow truck are on the way. I am, too."

Margo's heart pounded. Elmer was the town's rack-of-bones, eighty-nine-year-old icon who held court at the diner's back table from eight to nine every morning except Sunday. On the Lord's Day there was no grumbling about government on any level, the price of the morning paper or the proposed parking meters on Main Street. On Sunday, Elmer rested. He was a scrapper, as her dad used to say—and the hand-painted signs in the old bachelor's front yard attested to that. But he was *their* scrapper, and he had a heart of gold when it came to his friends. "Is he okay?"

"From what the tourist from Ohio said, I think so, but I can't say for sure. I guess he's pretty shaken up. He's got some cuts on his face."

Margo prayed he was right. "Okay, I'll get over there as soon as I can. Call Brett to assist."

"Will do."

She popped the tape out of her answering machine. "Take care of Elmer, Fish." Then, in spite of the rift between her and her Lord, she asked Him to watch over Elmer, too.

SEVEN

The rain was still coming down a full forty minutes later when Margo saw the first of three highway flares on Hawkins Road, but at least the storm had tapered off a little. "Thanks for driving," she said.

"No problem," Cole replied.

The scene was flooded with lights from Fish's cruiser, a fire truck and a few local firefighters' vehicles who'd also responded. Brett's SUV was there, too, and with flashlight in hand and dressed in the same department-issue yellow rain slicker Fish wore, he was moving light traffic along and directing the tow truck that was getting into position.

Cole pulled in behind the cruiser and Margo climbed out, tugging up the hood on her own yellow slicker. As she hurried toward Fish, rain drilled down on her head, nearly deafening against her hood.

"How's Elmer?" she called.

In his mid-twenties, the junior member of the department was tall and lanky, with dark eyes, a prominent nose and orthodontic braces. "I think he's okay. He gave the paramedics a rough time about being checked out at the hospital, but they took him anyway." Troutman flashed a mouthful of silver. "He'll probably want to sue."

That was encouraging. "So what happened?"

He nodded toward an SUV with Ohio plates. "Guy over there said Elmer wasn't driving all that fast, but it was too fast for conditions and he hydroplaned. Good thing he still drives that old relic. The dang thing's solid steel. I only called for a tow truck because the front fender got crushed against the wheel, and it can't be driven out of here."

Margo nodded. Elmer's '49 Ford truck was wedged into the side of a steep mud bank. It was a miracle that he'd missed the trees on either side of it. She walked over to the vehicle, took a minute to talk to Brett and the witness, then came back.

"Looks like you have things covered here, so I'll head to the hospital to talk to Elmer. See what his story is, and how he's doing."

"Better you than me. He's pretty ticked off."

Again, that was encouraging. He couldn't be badly hurt if he was giving everyone grief. "I'll see you tomorrow." With a wave to Brett, she returned to Cole's truck, shed her raincoat and tossed it in back before climbing inside. She'd thought about bringing Fish and Brett up-to-date on that message she'd received, but decided it could wait.

Before they'd left tonight—before Cole arrived at her house—she'd phoned Ellie Cortino. The cell phone number she'd supplied was a match to the number in Margo's caller ID window. The killer *had* called her home from Leanne's cell phone. Ellie had also provided the name of Leanne's cell service.

Then it was off to the station for a warrant and a quick drive to Judge Abbott's home. He'd signed the search warrant immediately. There'd been no glitches until she reached the carrier's emergency number. The techie who answered assured her they could get a satellite fix on the cell phone fairly quickly if it was turned on, but they needed documentation, and the legal department had to okay it. Unfortunately, there was no one in the legal department to approve their faxed search warrant on a Friday night after nine o'clock. No one would get the ball rolling until tomorrow.

Now pulling away from Elmer's accident scene, Cole drove toward town. "Are we going to the hospital or do you want to drop the tape off with the PSP?"

Margo massaged the tension on her forehead. "The hospital. I need to talk to Elmer."

"He's okay?"

"Fish thinks so."

Cole stared at the rain-streaked windshield and those swiftly moving wipers. "Looks like your living in the predigital Dark Ages paid off."

"How so?"

"You're still using your old answering machine. Easy access to the jerk's voice."

"True, but I'm not sure how helpful the tape will be without a sample to compare it to." She took a tissue from her navy windbreaker and daubed the rain from her face. "Our best bet is tracking the cell phone."

"Now let's hope the Hudson girl's carrier gets back to you first thing in the morning. Tonight, the rain kept him inside. Tomorrow could be a different story."

Margo didn't reply. The possibility that there could be another murder was too gruesome to contemplate. They needed the location of that phone.

After September 11, there'd been a demand for GPS chips to be placed in all cell phones. In 2005, they were accurate within one hundred meters. Now they could practically pinpoint a location. Cell phones had basically *become* tracking devices. In addition to the massive tracking network the National Security Agency had, wireless carriers offered services right now that let subscribers know with the touch of a button where their friends or families were.

Big Brother really was watching.

The rain had moved on by the time she and Cole left Elmer Fox in the hands of Charity General's nursing staff and headed back to Margo's house.

Leaning back against the headrest, Margo closed her eyes. She was positively drained, mentally and physically. She couldn't remember when she'd had six—even four—hours of uninterrupted sleep. According to novelist Robert Ludlum's Jason Bourne character, sleep was a weapon. If she didn't get some soon, she'd be running around unarmed.

She sank deeper into the seat, felt her breathing slow, felt her muscles relax. Flickering images danced behind her eyelids…a tapestry of fuzzy shapes and colors. She felt the breeze on her face from the Ferris wheel. Cole was smiling…telling her to hold on to him and she'd be safe.

Margo woke with a start as a pair of strong arms lifted her out of the truck and the night breeze blew across her cheek. "Cole? What are you—"

Nudging the door shut, he carried her up the steps to her porch.

"Put me down," she groaned, awake now. "I can walk."

"In a minute," he said, bending to unlock the door with the keys he'd obviously taken from her pocket.

Moments later, she was lying on her overstuffed blue sofa with a soft cream-and-blue throw pillow under her head, and looking up into the warmest brown eyes she'd ever known.

He sank to the cushion beside her. "Maybe you should sleep down here tonight. By the time you climb the stairs and get ready to turn in, you'll be wide-eyed and bushy tailed."

She sent him a groggy smile. She couldn't recall the last time she'd felt wide-eyed and bushy tailed...or the last time she'd felt so peaceful and pampered and cared for. How she'd missed this. "No, I'll go upstairs in a little while. Sorry about dozing off. I guess I wasn't much company on the way back from the hospital."

"No problem. After the day—and night—you had, you needed the rest."

Did she ever. "Thanks for chauffeuring me around."

"You're welcome. I just wish I could've done something to get things moving on that cell-phone trace. I don't like the idea of that freak calling you—and I don't get why he's doing it. Does he want to get caught? Or did he just want to needle you before he ditched the pho—" He stopped abruptly and softened his voice. "I'm sorry. I shouldn't have brought that up. Good luck tomorrow. I'll lock the door behind me."

"No, that's okay," she said, pushing herself up to walk him to the door. "I'll do it."

But Cole stayed where he was, and suddenly Margo found herself mere inches from the tenderness in his eyes...mere inches from his strong jaw, his perfect mouth. It was a distance neither of them could ignore.

Margo drew a soft breath as Cole's fingers slid through her hair to coax her forward. Then he covered her lips with his own, the kiss a gentle, healing balm that nearly made her forget the fears and ugliness of the past few days. It made her heart swell and her eyes tear.

She knew it couldn't last. This was only temporary, just a little respite brought about by weariness, nature and nightfall. Tomorrow things would return to normal and his kiss would be just another memory she could tuck away. But for tonight…tonight, she could pretend it was forever.

Finally, Cole eased away, a hint of regret marring his rugged features. But regret for what, Margo didn't know. "I'll talk to you tomorrow sometime," he said. "Sleep tight."

"I'll try," she murmured. But how could she sleep when all she wanted was to stay here with him in this moment and not think about anything else?

Bolting upright, Margo shut off her shrieking, beeping alarm clock and looked at the time: 8:00 a.m. It took her a second to clear her head. Then she remembered why she wanted to be in the office by nine on what should've been her day off. She was awaiting word that Hudson's wireless carrier had located the victim's cell phone. Another memory surfaced, one that was equally emotional. Cole would be well on his way to Pittsburgh now, if he hadn't already arrived. He'd be catching up on his work, getting ready for his "dinner."

Margo shook off a jealous twinge and got out of bed—crossed to the window facing her backyard and the steep hills beyond. Reaching under the ruffled white organdy curtains with the tiny pink embroidered roses, she raised the blind and opened the window wide, letting in the sunshine and fresh air. There was no trace of the heavy humidity they'd been dealing with for the past week, and not a drop of rain in sight. The sky was a brilliant blue, scrubbed clean by last night's storm. Above the shaded hills, huge cotton-ball clouds drifted along, edged in sunlight.

There was a time when her first thought upon waking was to thank God for a peaceful night and praise Him for a beautiful morning. She missed that. And today He'd outdone Himself. Suddenly she was reminded of Noah's ark, and the beautiful rainbow God had sent to let Noah know the storm was over. Noah had released a dove then, and it had returned to the ark with an olive branch…the sign of peace.

Funny… She hadn't thought of that story for years. Had God put that thought in her head to send a message? She didn't know. She did know it would be hard to stay mad at Him on a day like today.

Crossing to the phone on her nightstand, Margo called Sarah at the station to fill her in on the night's events. "And Sarah," she added. "Let me know the second you hear from the carrier. I'll be in by nine or so. If I'm not there when the call comes in, you can reach me on my cell phone."

"Will do," she replied, then went on. "Honey, I thought you were off today."

"I was. See you soon."

Her next call was personal. The news she received from Lila Essex at the nurses' station was totally unexpected. Charity's favorite octogenarian had been discharged. Except for some bruises, a slight concussion and a cut on his forehead from hitting the steering wheel, he'd been given a clean bill of health. Amazingly, he'd suffered no fractures. But Elmer's truck wouldn't be usable for a while, Charity didn't have a taxi service and the hospital was more than four miles from Elmer's home. That concerned her.

"Did Elmer catch a ride, Lila?"

"Why, yes, he did," she replied in a teasing singsong. "An old friend of yours stopped by a few minutes ago to visit, then drove him home."

"An old friend of mine?"

"Yep. He was about six-two and gorgeous, needs a haircut, but Doreen and I hope he skips it. And he was wearing an off-white collarless knit shirt tucked into dark jeans. Oh, and brown cowboy boots. Of course," she continued laughing, "we really didn't get a good look at him."

Margo had to laugh, too.

Just then, someone spoke in the background, and Lila amended her report. "Margo, Doreen said they were headed for the diner, not Elmer's place. You might be able to catch them there."

"Thanks, Lila. I'll do that."

Quickly showering and drying her hair, Margo sorted through her closet for something slightly feminine but sensible since she'd be working part of the day. She decided on polished blue chinos, and a three-quarter sleeve white wrap-blouse with a mandarin collar and shirring at the shoulders. Then she added white sandals and gold hoop earrings.

She grabbed her keys, tucked her cell phone into her shoulder bag and stepped out on the front porch. Ignoring the morning paper near the door, she skipped down the stairs and drove toward town.

Handling the murder case and taking over John's duties had eaten up so much of her time these past two weeks, she'd had to curtail most of life's simple pleasures. This morning, barring another surprise, she'd get to enjoy at least two of them: a breakfast she didn't have to make

herself, and conversations with a man she admired...
and a man she loved.

The diner's bouncy music wasn't nearly as intrusive as
it had been the other day when she'd stopped by. In fact,
it was invigorating. Families were clustered around the
center tables that had been pushed together, and most of
the booths were taken. Her heart sank as she spotted the
table that was Elmer Fox's between the hours of eight
and nine. It had been commandeered by another group.
She looked around the restaurant, hoping that Cole and
Elmer might've settled for one of the booths, but no.

The diner's owner left the lunch counter and crossed
to where Margo stood, flat-footed and disappointed, in
the middle of the eatery. Aggie Benson was a white-
haired charmer with a pixie cut, twinkling blue eyes
and a perennial smile she carried around on a round,
five-foot-no-inch frame.

"They left a little while ago," she said.

"Who?"

A bit of humor touched her voice. "Obviously, the two
men you're looking for. Cole took Elmer home. Despite
all his blathering to the contrary, he was tired, and Cole
saw it."

"He's all right, though?"

"He is. He's a tough old turkey, but the man's eighty-
nine years old. He's entitled to an off day after a late-
night disagreement with a mud bank." She nodded toward
an empty booth. "How about some breakfast? Or maybe
you'd rather get going? Maybe there's somewhere else
you want to be?"

Margo smiled and shook her head. What was going
on? Two of the three people she'd spoken with today were
into teasing lines and secret grins. "You're right, Aggie.
I do have somewhere I need to be. The station."

"I didn't say *need*," she returned, chuckling and heading for the coffee carafes behind the lunch counter. "I said *want*. I'll get you a decaf to go." She was nearly there when she turned and lowered her voice. "Any news yet on the...you know?"

Margo shook her head. How she wished there were.

A minute later, she'd paid for her coffee and was walking toward her red Cherokee when she stopped cold. A man who could've been Ray Masters had just exited the hardware store next to the bank and was now getting into a silver SUV.

Adrenaline pumping, Margo hurried to her car, hopped inside and started the engine. If that *was* Masters, what was he doing in Charity? Determined to find out, she drove to the exit, then groaned when the red light up the street blinked on, stopping traffic and blocking her in. To her further chagrin, an Amish buggy clopped into line behind the last vehicle.

It wasn't unusual to see Amish folks in town. There was a small community on the outskirts of Charity. But today, following behind a horse and buggy wasn't in the best interests of the Charity P.D.

By the time she was able to pull around the buggy and drive up the street to the state route beyond, the silver SUV was long gone. There was nothing for her to do but return to town and see Ben Caruthers at the hardware store.

In his sixties and balding, with kind eyes that matched the gray in his plaid shirt, he smiled at her from behind the counter.

"Yes, I waited on him," he said when she asked. "I didn't know him, but he paid cash, so there was no need to ask for identification."

"What did he buy, Ben?"

"Not much. A couple of drill bits and a hundred feet of rope. He wanted a cell-phone battery, but I don't carry much in the line of electronics. He did buy one of those generic cell phones, though. You know," he said, pointing to a spinner rack. "That kind over there in the blister pack. The kind you have to buy minutes for."

His mention of cell phones made her uneasy until logic stepped in. Ropes and scarves were very different accessories, and the Gold Star Killer's M.O. hadn't varied. Also, the carnival's manager *had* mentioned that he couldn't reach Masters on his cell the other day, so there was nothing suspicious about a man trying to replace a dead battery or opting for a generic phone.

But if the person she'd seen was Masters, why would he drive forty miles to buy standard items he could've purchased in Laurel Banks? The only reason she could come up with was petty, but it was definitely in line with Masters's personality. Maybe he just felt like stirring the pot. Maybe he hoped he'd be spotted in a town where he wasn't welcome.

"If I see the guy again, I'll give you a call," Ben said, obviously trying to be helpful when Margo stayed too long in her thoughts.

"Thanks," she replied. "I'd appreciate that. But if he's who I think he is, he won't be back." The carnival would be pulling up stakes and moving on tomorrow, and Masters would be going with it. "See you later, Ben."

"Going to the church picnic?" he called after her.

She paused at the door, feeling a nostalgic tug. Even though she and God weren't on the best of terms, she did miss the gatherings and the warm friendships she found at the church's functions. But right now she couldn't be sure of anything. If all went well, she could be processing a prisoner tomorrow—or even better, today. "I'm not sure. I'm working until two."

"Well, we're not eatin' until three, so try to join us."

"I might do that. Thanks, Ben. See you."

She was halfway across the street when Cole pulled into a parking space to the left of the station. Feeling an airy little lift, she walked across the street to meet him.

"Good morning," he called, getting out and waiting for her.

"Good morning to you, too." Doreen and Lila were right. Nice, civilized haircuts looked great on some men. But Cole Blackburn wasn't some men. He was one of a kind. The slightly shaggy, wind-tossed look suited him.

He dropped his voice as they drew closer. "How did you sleep?"

"Like the dead. Better than I have in weeks."

"I'm not surprised. You've been putting in some full days. Any word from the girl's carrier yet?"

"Not yet, but I'm hopeful we'll hear something soon. Speaking of putting in full days, I understand you picked up Elmer this morning at the hospital."

"Yeah, I did. He wanted to go to the diner for breakfast before I took him home, but he was really wiped out. He put up a good front for a while, though." He grinned. "No one can say he's not entertaining."

"That's for sure. Did he tell you he thinks the FBI's tapping his phone?"

The skin beside his dark eyes crinkled with his smile. "No, but after seeing all those signs in his front yard, I can believe it."

Margo smiled back, glad to have something to smile

about, glad to be smiling with *him.* "I thought you were heading back to Pittsburgh early this morning."

"I was, but I wanted to make sure Elmer had what he needed before I took off." He paused. "I wanted to see you, too." Margo's momentary high fizzled when he continued. "I meant to pick up the Gold Star folder when I took you home last night but I forgot."

"Oh. I didn't see it. Where did you put it?"

"I slid it under the sofa in your living room before we left. Do you mind if I pick it up before I leave? If I have some downtime before dinner, I can look through it again."

She really wished he'd stop talking about that dinner unless he was willing to elaborate. "Sure." She wiggled her house key off her ring. "I have a spare. Just let yourself in."

"Thanks. I'll give it back to you tomorrow." He frowned then, dark thoughts moving through his eyes. "I won't ask you to bunk at your mother's place or invite a friend to stay over. I know you won't do it. I've already heard your 'guns trump scarves' speech. But at the risk of sounding like a broken record, watch your step, okay?"

"I will," she returned. "Have a safe trip."

"Thanks. See you soon."

Margo walked up the steps to the station and went inside. She didn't wait for him to pull out. Strange, how time changed things. Over a year ago, she'd tried to make him see that the two of them could still have a life together—in their dream home. In the community he'd come to love. All he had to do was commute between Charity and Pittsburgh a few times a week. He'd turned the idea down flat. Now he was doing it by choice.

All except the part about their having a life together.

She'd barely sat down to schedule next week's officer coverage when Sarah called to her. "Margo, Cole's on line one. He says it's important."

Poking the flashing button, Margo picked up. "Cole?"

His voice couldn't have been any graver. "I'm at your place. I think you might want to join me. You'll need gloves, an evidence bag, a fingerprint kit and a camera. I'll stay put. Chain of evidence."

Margo's heartbeat stepped up its pace. "What's going on?"

"I'm pretty sure you can forget about the trace on Hudson's cell phone. The killer doesn't have it anymore. I think it's in your mailbox."

EIGHT

Cole plunged his hands in his pockets as he walked around the PSP's asphalt lot, his Silverado parked next to Margo's Cherokee—though not with her blessing. She'd tried to dissuade him from coming along, reminded him that he had plans in Pittsburgh. But he needed to hang around for a while. Knowing the killer could've been on her front porch had turned his gut to jelly.

He glanced at the imposing redbrick edifice. Margo was inside now, dropping off the tape and that smashed pink cell phone he'd found in her mailbox. He'd only intended to take the newspaper and the day's mail in since he was going inside for the file folder anyway. Then...surprise, surprise.

Obviously the phone wasn't going to transmit a signal with the battery gone and all of its working parts reduced to bits of scrap metal. But it was the right color and brand to be Leanne Hudson's phone, and that was good enough for now. Hopefully, the lab could piece it together and come up with a partial print or fibers that could be matched later.

He was working on his twentieth slow walk around the parking lot when Margo stepped outside, shared a few parting words with an officer, then shook his hand and walked back to their vehicles.

"What's the verdict?" he asked. "Was there enough to work with?"

"Maybe. It'll be days until they know, though." She paused. "Now, go home. Get ready for your dinner date. Unless you've already canceled?"

He narrowed his gaze on her. Was she fishing? He hadn't mentioned it being a date—though he guessed it qualified as one, even though the woman was Sherry. "No, I didn't. She's being honored for her volunteer work with abused women. I can't bow out."

"Oh," Margo replied. "She sounds special."

Was that disappointment or disinterest in her voice? Some days it was hard to tell. All he knew was the part of him still stinging from the breakup—the petty part—wanted her to know that some women still found him attractive. "She's a good friend. I want to be there to honor her work, but at the same time, things are getting sticky around here."

She searched his eyes for a moment, then slipped inside her ride—spoke through the open window. "I'll handle it. You need to get going."

"We need to talk first."

"About?"

"About your having a home security alarm installed—and about your staying at Jenna's place for a while." She started to protest, and he held up a staying hand. "Margo, he knows where you live."

"No."

"Fine," he returned, irritated. "Then buy yourself a filmy nightgown and a few candles, because it looks like you're determined to trot up the stone steps to the attic to see what that creepy noise was."

Margo sighed at his reference to gothic films with idiotic heroines. "Cole, I'm the acting chief of police. I wouldn't have a snowball's chance of getting the permanent position if I cut and ran. What kind of confidence would that inspire? I'll be fine. I'm well trained, and I know what I'm doing."

The words *permanent position* rang in his ears, rang in his mind—did something tricky to his stomach. "You're also a woman."

"I'll pretend you didn't say that."

"Don't. Then I'd have to repeat it. This bozo hates women, and he's already hinted that you could be his next target. Not taking steps to insure your safety is lunacy." He dropped his voice. "If it was Jenna—not you—who'd been threatened, you'd move heaven and earth to see that she was protected. That's all I'm trying to do."

She fell silent for a moment, her defensiveness ebbing. Then she combed her fingers through her silky hair, and moistened her lips. "Would you run away if you were the lead investigator on this case?"

Cole blew out an impatient breath. No, he wouldn't, but telling her that wouldn't be productive. "We're not talking about me. This jerk kills women, not men. I don't want you to be his next victim."

"I won't be. I have steel doors, excellent locks and I sleep with a gun on my nightstand. Besides, he preys on women who walk alone after dark. He attacks them in the park. We both know that killers rarely change their M.O.'s."

Cole crouched down, met her eye to eye. "When coyotes run out of rabbits and other small prey, they expand their territory. Women aren't walking in the park after dark anymore. From what I've heard, it's practically deserted after six o'clock. If your coyote needs to hunt and there are no more rabbits in his neck of the woods, he's going to look elsewhere—possibly toward a rabbit who's already ticked him off." He sighed. "Now, please, go to Jenna's tonight. You can use my room."

"I can't do that."

The words came out more sharply than he'd intended. "Because you want the chief position so badly?"

"Because I'm being paid to do a job."

"Then get an alarm system. A lot of them are relatively inexpensive. Grayson Security does a good job."

He watched her insert the key, start the Cherokee's engine…and finally, agree. "All right. I'll look into it on Monday. Now, stop browbeating me and go home. You have plans, and I have things to do."

Straightening, Cole waited until she was under way, then walked to his truck and opened the door. He watched her brake lights flicker briefly before she pulled onto the main road, felt that nerve in his jaw throb.

Monday was a long way off.

Pulling his cell phone from the case on his belt, he climbed inside and slid behind the wheel—tapped in a number and waited. She wasn't going to be happy about this, but…

A cheerful feminine voice answered. "Blackberry Hill Bed and Breakfast. This is Jenna."

"Jenna, it's Cole Blackburn. Are you busy tonight?"

The moment Margo looked outside and saw Jenna in the side-spill of the front porch's motion lights, she knew exactly who was responsible for Jenna's unexpected late-night visit. And he was going to hear about it. Pulling back the spring-loaded dead bolt, she opened the door.

"Jenna," she said, smiling and accepting the warm

dish Jenna placed in her hands. "Come in." As usual, her friend looked cover-girl perfect in lemon-yellow slacks and a white, short-sleeved sweater edged in yellow. Gold hoop earrings peeked out from her shoulder-length, dark blond hair, and a tiny gold cross hung from a chain around her neck. Margo hid a wry smile. *She* was wearing burgundy sweatpants and a gray Charity P.D. T-shirt.

Margo nudged the door shut. The dead bolt slid back into place.

"Sorry about the late hour," her friend said, "but you weren't home earlier."

No, she wasn't. She'd gone to the carnival to talk with Ray Masters. "What brings you down from the hill?"

Jenna had a wonderful laugh, belying the trouble she'd run from. "Would you believe I had so much apple cobbler left over from breakfast, I suddenly wanted to share it with a friend?"

"No, I wouldn't, but it smells great so I'm glad you're here." She nodded for Jenna to precede her into the kitchen.

Nudging her floral centerpiece aside, Margo set the cobbler in the middle of the table. "Cole called you, didn't he? He asked you to come over here and Margo-sit."

"Yes. But don't be upset. He's worried. He doesn't want you to be alone while he's out of town."

Margo pulled dessert plates, cups and saucers from a cupboard, then faced Jenna again, hoping her weariness didn't show. "Why should he care? I'm going to be alone for months—years—when he goes back for good. Is he planning to show up every time he thinks I need his help, then afterward, ride off into the sunset again?"

She arranged the dishes on the table, added silverware from a drawer. "He kissed me last night, Jen. But tonight he's taking another woman to dinner—someone special who's being honored for her work with abused women. I can't compete with that." She plucked a few paper napkins from the holder and put them on the table.

Jenna took a chair. "Is he kissing her, too?"

"I don't know, and it's making me crazy. And I can't very well ask him."

"Why not?"

Margo's jaw sagged. Then shaking her head, she filled the kettle and set it on to boil. "He said they're friends."

"Did you believe him?"

"He's never lied to me, so yes, I guess I did."

Jenna peeled the foil from the cobbler. "Then maybe that's all there is to it."

"Maybe," Margo repeated. But sometimes friendships became more, and the thought of that made her chest ache and her throat tight. A change of subject was in order. Gathering tea bags and condiments, she took them to the oak table. "So, who's minding the store tonight while you're here with me?"

Jenna's blue eyes warmed. "Aunt Molly. She loves stepping in from time to time. She got all dressed up in one of her period costumes for the occasion."

Jenna's eighty-year-old great-aunt had owned and run the Blackberry for fifty years before turning it over to Jenna eight months ago. Margo suspected she'd still be running the historic inn, but arthritis had stepped in and made the decision that Molly Jennings couldn't. "Sounds like she misses it."

"She does—and our returning guests miss *her*. They loved her vintage dresses and cameo pins." After a brief hesitation, she slid their paper napkins close, then slowly folded them into perfect triangles. "I told her I'd be home before the guests came down for breakfast."

Margo went stone still. She'd thought this was just a pop-in-and-make-sure-Margo's-okay visit. "Jenna, believe me, I'm glad to have your company anytime, and I thank you for caring, but you have a business to run. You don't have time for a slumber party."

"Aunt Molly will be fine. She doesn't have to do a thing except be there. You're my friend. The best one I have. Cole's not the only one who worries."

"But you don't have to, and neither does he. If I can't take care of myself, I have no business wearing a badge." She felt her initial irritation return. "Oh, he's really going to hear it."

The teakettle whistled. Margo turned off the burner and carried the kettle to the table. Jenna's lovely blue gaze reflected the darkness she'd had to deal with.

"Margo, I know about this kind of thing. I have the scar to prove it."

Margo nodded gravely as she poured hot water into their cups. Jenna had left Michigan when a man she'd dated several times turned into a knife-wielding stalker. But that was all she knew about that time in her friend's life. Jenna didn't talk about it.

"Okay, I'll admit to being uneasy. But I've had plenty of time to think about how this jerk operates. Obviously, I'm not a profiler but certain things make sense to me from an investigative perspective. If he's been on my porch—close enough to do some damage—but all he did was drop a gift in my mailbox, he's not interested in hurting me." The note, the message on her answering machine, the smashed phone... She'd begun to think it was all a game to him.

She focused on the only certain fact they knew about

the killer as she returned the kettle to the stove. "I think he's playing with me because he considers women weak. Seeing me show fear would give him a big ego boost, a sense of power that—maybe—he doesn't have in his day-to-day life. The game stops if I'm gone."

Jenna's expression said she didn't like any of it. "I hope you're right."

Margo hoped she was, too. The fact remained that those were just her thoughts. She handed a serving spoon to Jenna. "If it makes you feel better, I'll be calling someone about home security on Monday."

"It does."

"Great. Now, let's eat."

When their plates were filled, Jenna took both of Margo's hands across the table. "Blessed Lord," she said, "thank You for this food, and for the many blessings You've given us. Thank You, too, for my friend Margo, who needs your grace and guidance now. Please keep her safe as she does her job, and when this horror is resolved, give her what she needs to be happy."

Margo felt her eyes sting as she added her own petitions. "Bless my friend Jenna, as well. She's dealt with some difficult things. Please keep her safe, too."

"Amen," they said together, then shared a smile.

"Okay," Jenna said, removing her tea bag and adding sugar. "If you won't let me stay the night, at least tell me that there's an officer standing by if there's trouble."

"Fish is on tonight, so he'll drive by a few times while he's on patrol. If I need him, he's only a few minutes away." Margo sampled her cobbler and smiled. "This is wonderful. Not too sweet, not too tart."

"Thanks. Glad you like it." Jenna filled her fork. "I just wish you had a few leads. Then you'd know who to watch."

Earlier today, she'd thought she might have a lead. But Ray Masters didn't own a silver SUV, and every carney she questioned swore Masters had never left the grounds this morning. Once again, trying to link Masters to the crime had been a waste of time. She'd come home wanting to discuss her failed trip with Cole, but she knew it would've only been an excuse to hear his voice and ruin his date.

Jenna was still waiting for an answer.

"This morning, I thought I saw a man we'd questioned before coming out of the hardware store. A drifter with a criminal record and tons of attitude. Shortly after I saw him, the phone showed up in my mailbox, so I drove to his location to question him again."

"Alone?"

"We're a small department, Jen. Everyone's working at least two double shifts a week right now. I couldn't take an officer off duty to go on what could've been a witch hunt."

"Was it?"

"With this guy, who knows? He said he never left his trailer this morning. But when I asked if he was sure he hadn't been to my house, he laughed and said he couldn't have. He didn't know where I lived. He said I'm not in the phone book."

"Which he wouldn't have known unless he'd checked." Jenna shook her head. "Know what? If I were you—"

The phone rang.

Jenna's gaze went to the wall phone, then returned to Margo.

"Don't worry," she said, pushing away from the table. "It's probably just a telemarketer. They're like Energizer Bunnies. They never quit. They call at mealtimes, on

Sundays, on holidays, when I'm in the shower.... But, I guess a job's a job."

But it wasn't a telemarketer, Ray Masters or the boogeyman. It was Cole's cell number in the ID window. Margo picked up the receiver and spoke coolly before he could say a word. "You're in a lot of trouble, mister."

An hour after Jenna left, Margo took a shower, folded her tea-roses bedspread down to the foot of the bed and climbed in. As promised, she grabbed her phone and tapped in Cole's number. He answered immediately.

"Okay, I'm in bed and everything's secure. There are marines behind every bush and tree, two helicopters in the air and Gil Grissom's entire CSI lab is waiting to process the scene in case the good guys slip up."

"Don't joke about that," he said, annoyed. "Is Jenna with you?"

"No," she said firmly. "I told you she wasn't staying when I spoke to you earlier. Now, please. This has to stop. Sending Jenna here tells me that you don't trust my judgment, you don't respect my training and you doubt my abilities. I don't like it."

He didn't say anything for a long moment, but she could hear soft jazz in the background, so she knew he was still on the line. He liked Miles Davis.

"Okay," he said finally. "I'm officially backing off. What you do about your safety is your own business. Is anything else going on?"

Obviously, this wasn't a good time to mention her discussion with Ray Masters. "Nothing productive. We're still looking for Chase Merritt and still waiting for forensics to report on Leanne's cell phone. I just wish Merritt had a cell." She'd been startled to learn that he didn't. "We could've tried to track him, too."

"Okay. I'm going to sign off and get some sleep so I can be back for church in the morning. Will I see you there?"

"No, Charlie and I are covering until O'Dell comes in at two."

"What about the picnic?"

"I'm not sure. Maybe—"

"Know what?" he said crisply. "You're building a life around that word. It's as if you can't commit to *any*thing. If you're at the picnic, I'll see you there. If not, I'll talk to you sometime on Monday after I look over the year-books. Have a good night."

"Wait!" she said. "I was going to say that maybe I could make potato salad on my lunch—" Margo halted, looked at the phone, then brought it to her ear again. "Cole? Are you there?" Rapid beeping sounded in her earpiece followed by a recorded voice telling her that if she'd like to make a call, she should hang up and try again.

She slammed down the receiver. What was *that* flare-up all about? He couldn't be that bent out of shape because she'd sent Jenna home—not when he'd just agreed to back off. It had to be something else.

She'd heard a talk-show psychologist say something interesting a few years ago. He'd said that some arguments had nothing to do with the current problem. Well, if that's what this was, she wasn't going to give herself a headache trying to figure it out.

Margo glanced at the book lying on her nightstand, the statistical book on serial killers that she'd brought upstairs earlier. The book right next to her Glock. Ignoring it, she clicked off her lamp, deciding that some books were better read in the daylight hours.

She turned on her side, stared through her open

window, listened to the coyotes yipping and calling to the thin crescent moon. It had lost its luster, and some cloud cover remained. But the night was still and beautiful, and all of a sudden, Margo felt terribly alone...and missing that deep connection to her Creator.

Cole stood in the window of his fifth-floor apartment, looking out at the city. It was pretty at night—all lit up like a Christmas tree. Located on the floor above the Sharp Investigations offices, his small efficiency had once hosted a number of P.I.'s who'd worked late, then didn't feel like braving winter storms or city traffic. Now it was his exclusively. Head honcho Clete Banning had dangled it like a carrot when Cole refused his first offer to join their team. Free digs in the middle of prime Pittsburgh real estate more than made up for the money he'd lost.

He wandered over to the CD player where Miles Davis was playing some of the best jazz he'd ever heard, but wasn't appreciating. He turned it off and heard her voice again.

"Cole, I'm the acting chief of police. I wouldn't have a snowball's chance of getting the permanent position if I cut and ran."

That's all he'd thought about all night—and that included the time he'd spent with Sherry, though she probably hadn't noticed. The crowd from SWAN—Stop Women's Abuse Now—had been warmly attentive to their chief fundraiser, and rightly so. But— There was always a "but," wasn't there? His mind had been on Margo and their on again, off again history. Luckily, he wasn't interested in repeating it. Because this time, it would be her job that ended it. She couldn't be Charity's chief of police if she lived in Pittsburgh.

Cole turned off the lamps and walked to his bedroom, distant city lights finding their way into the shadows and showing the way. *Maybe, maybe, maybe.* Not one of his favorite words.

Maybe they should wait to be married until he found another job. *Maybe* she shouldn't move to Pittsburgh until he knew P.I. work suited him. And *maybe* they could postpone their wedding until her mother was able to cope.

Well, her mother was better, but the top job in the Charity Police Department was now on the table. Even if he wanted her back, which he didn't...

Maybe it was a waste of time to pursue it.

NINE

The late-Sunday-morning sun shone brightly, glancing off one, then a second news van pulling into the convenience store's blacktopped lot. Stifling a groan, Margo pushed through the plate-glass door, nodded to the two emerging reporters, then carried her lunch—a vanilla milk shake—to her waiting prowl car.

They converged on her at the same time. One was a young guy from a Pittsburgh station who was probably still making his bones, and the other was unrelenting Johnstown News hound, Nancy Talbot. She and her black eyeliner nudged the competition out of the way and strode forward, her voice as crisp as Margo remembered.

"Chief McBride, it's been five days since the Hudson girl was killed. Area residents see this as a red-letter day since there were five days between the first two murders. Are you feeling even more apprehensive today, knowing that this vicious serial killer could strike again tonight?"

Margo sent her a disbelieving look. Once again, she'd thrown responsible reporting out the window, and resorted to tabloid journalism. There was no doubt that Talbot's style would get her a lot of attention. But this kind of reckless reporting escalated people's fears.

It took willpower to answer calmly when all Margo wanted to do was run the woman out of town. "We're not placing any more importance on this day than we did on previous days. We're continuing to follow the evidence and, along with the Pennsylvania State Police, are working to find the killer."

"Are you saying you don't believe that Day Five is important?"

Day Five? Dear God.

Talbot pressed on. "Serial killers have been known to act on nights when the moon is full, or certain days of the week, or—"

"The moon isn't full, and if our killer had taken a liking to a certain day, he'd want to be active on Tuesday."

Talbot kept nodding in an effort to hurry her along. "True, but I wasn't finished. You must know that some serial killers have an affinity for numbers."

"And some act randomly," Margo replied curtly.

The woman's eyes flashed in indignation, then she reacted to Margo's tone in kind, zeroing in on her Achilles' heel. "What are your personal thoughts about the case right now, ma'am? With nothing new and very few leads, you have to be feeling utterly frustrated—even powerless. Have you considered that it might be time to turn the investigation over to someone with more experience? Doesn't the family deserve better?"

Talbot's verbal blow hit Margo like a sledgehammer. She *was* frustrated, and at times, she did feel powerless. But people were depending on her, and she had to demonstrate confidence. It took all of her fortitude to keep her expression smooth and her tone professional.

"The family deserves the very best that law enforcement can provide. That's exactly what they're getting from our department and from the state police. As for my personal feelings, my heart aches for all of the families. That's why I'm determined to get results."

The reporter from Pittsburgh thrust a microphone at her. His keen gaze was just as sharp as Talbot's, but at least he wasn't wearing black eyeliner, and he got her title right. She was glad she already had her guard up, because his first question jolted her, and brought a startled look to Talbot's features.

"Officer McBride, Rob Curtain, Eye on the City News. Channel 93 has learned that you received a note the day after the murder that might've come from the killer. Can you tell us what the note said? And has there been any further communication from him?"

Wonderful. Despite the fact that she'd asked everyone to keep the note quiet, they had a leak. Well, she wouldn't lie. Lies, like chickens, always came home to roost. Still, she wouldn't give the killer a reason to gloat.

"Yes, there was a note, but it was basically nothing. We doubt it even came from the killer."

Curtain cocked his head. "If not from the killer, then who?"

"Someone who wants attention. The world is full of people who need to be noticed. Unfortunately for that person, we decided not to feed his ego and make the note public. I'm sorry you brought it up. Where did you get this information, Mr. Curtain?"

He rattled off the expected response. "From a source close to the investigation who prefers to remain anonymous."

"You can do better than that."

"No. I'm sorry, I can't."

"All right." Margo opened the cruiser's door and sent Curtain a level look. "I hope your source isn't a person of interest in this case. If he is and we find out about it, I won't only be talking to you. I'll be talking to your station manager."

Three hours later, with her pride still battered and bruised, Margo pulled into the church's lot—and rolled her eyes skyward. The Channel 29 news van was there. Wasn't someone or something making news somewhere other than Charity?

Squaring her shoulders and wondering what she'd done to God today, Margo climbed the stairs, then veered to the right and followed the music to the grassy, festively decorated churchyard. She placed the potato salad she'd made during her lunch hour on a table flanked by blue-and-white streamers and bobbing balloons in a variety of colors. Then she glanced around.

Sure enough, Nancy Talbot was a dozen yards away, facing her cameraman and speaking loudly enough to be overheard by curious onlookers. When she heard Talbot's lead-in, Margo wanted to pop the woman with her own microphone. Not a very Christian thought, but at least it was honest.

"We're here in the small town of Charity, Pennsylvania," Talbot intoned somberly, "where the congregation of Saint John's Church has come together in prayer and fellowship, trying to blot out the horror of the past week. But can they? Many residents fear that on this fifth day since the murder—"

Margo couldn't listen anymore. Spotting friends and a few others talking near the soft-drinks table—one of whom was a tall, broad-shouldered man in jeans and a blue polo shirt—Margo started across the grass to join them. He was probably still miffed, and that was fine. She was, too. She was still glad she'd shed her uniform for a pretty black sundress dotted with tiny Victorian roses and trimmed in narrow white-eyelet.

As she drew near, she heard Jenna introduce their good friend Rachel Patterson to three strangers. One of them, a young woman in her mid to late twenties with long, luxuriously silky black hair, had eyes only for Cole.

Margo yanked the pins out of her bun and shook her hair loose.

"Hi," she said, getting their attention. "Nice day."

Cole looked her way and nodded politely, but it pleased her that he checked out her dress. She sent him a cool nod back.

"Yes, it is," Jenna returned. "Margo, I'd like you to meet my guests, Don and Nora Florio from Bridgeport, Connecticut, and their daughter Cheryl. Cheryl just earned her doctorate in psychology, so her folks are treating her to a trip."

"How nice," Margo said, shaking hands all around.

"Someone mentioned the county's huge elk herd," Jenna went on, "and they'd like to take a peek. I suggested they drive down to Rachel's place in the valley— possibly stay in one of her tourist cabins overnight."

"Unfortunately, my cabins are full right now," their slender brunette friend replied. "But if you get there just before daybreak, you're sure to see them. They're not shy. They stroll right through the campground."

"Actually," Cole said, "I was there earlier this morning, and spotted a few bulls. Their velvet's gone, and they're starting to bugle."

Margo looked away. Why did everything he did without her now hurt so much? Once upon a time, they'd grabbed their cameras and gone looking for elk together. But no more. She was relieved when talk turned to other points of interest and she was able to beg off and mingle.

Rachel fell into step beside her, her razor-cut sable hair and deep bangs shining in the sunlight. The airy, pink-and-white floral, off-the-shoulder voile sundress she wore was a surprise. Margo was used to seeing her in a camp shirt and jeans. Since her husband's death two years ago, Rachel ran their rustic restaurant and cabin business alone.

She spoke tentatively. "Speaking of points of interest…I couldn't help noticing that Cheryl seems to have found one that she likes."

Margo sent her a sarcastic look. "That's an understatement. If she moves any closer to him they'll be standing back-to-back."

"You're fine with that? With your history?"

"Of course." There was no point looking like a jealous teen-queen when the woman was only passing through. "He's a good-looking man. She'd have to be blind not to notice. And if he's interested in her—so be it."

"He's not. Every time she moved closer, he backed up." Rachel laughed softly. "At least that's how it went until you showed up."

Margo didn't reply, but a little teen-queen satisfaction did make its way into her smile.

Up ahead, past the strolling clowns and kids trailing balloons and blowing soap bubbles, she spotted a spry old man with a bandaged forehead. From the smiles and chuckles of those gathered around his picnic table, he was apparently spinning another yarn. "Let's go see how Elmer's doing, okay?"

"Good idea," Rachel replied, concern etching her brow. "I'm glad he's doing all right. Patty Grimes said she heard the responders had to use the Jaws of Life to get Elmer out of his truck."

Margo grinned wryly. Small towns just couldn't help embellishing an already great story. "Actually, he got out of the truck on his own. But now that I think about it, Elmer could be the guy starting the stories. I'll let him tell you what happened."

It was going on seven o'clock, the crowd had dwindled and Margo was helping the ladies of the auxiliary strip the paper tablecloths from the tables when Cole wandered over to her, carrying a trash bag.

"Nice dress."

Margo pulled up the paper and stuffed it in the bag. "Thanks."

"I had some of your potato salad. It was good."

"Glad you enjoyed it. How did Miss Bridgeport, Connecticut, like it?"

A smile entered his voice. "I believe that's Doctor Bridgeport, Connecticut. And I think she skipped it. Are you jealous?"

"Are you hoping?" She moved to the next table. "There's a new wrinkle in the case."

His amusement disappeared. "What's going on?"

"We have a leak. Either in our department or the PSP's. A Pittsburgh reporter waylaid me outside the Quick Stop this morning. He knows about the 'back off' note."

"He wasn't just fishing?"

"No. Now I'm wondering who blabbed. Charlie swears he didn't breathe a word to anyone. Steve was insulted that I'd even ask, and the others aren't in today." She finally met his eyes. She didn't really believe he'd leaked the information, but she sent him a questioning look, anyway. Not because he'd eaten with the Florio family. Because he hadn't eaten with her.

Cole didn't mince words. "It wasn't me, and I think you know that."

Margo moved to the last table. "Any ideas?"

"Just one."

"Care to share?"

Sighing, Cole stopped her hands as she started to rip up the paper, then tipped her chin up to meet his eyes. "I'm sorry about last night on the phone. I was short with you."

"Yes, you were. Why?"

He shook his head. "I don't know. Just…stuff. It doesn't matter."

Yes, it did, but if he didn't want to explain, it was probably best that she didn't know. She lost the attitude. She'd never been very good at it, anyway. "It's okay. We all get short sometimes. I wanted to pop a reporter today."

"Yeah? Why?"

She smiled a little and quoted his words. "Just…stuff. It doesn't matter. Let's move on." She stripped the paper from the table and shoved it in the bag. "I asked if you had any ideas of who the leak could be. You said just one. Who?"

"The killer," he said grimly. "I think we should go somewhere quiet and discuss it."

Humming happily to himself, he crossed the frayed carpeting to the motel's cheap writing desk, the little ditty running through his mind, one he'd learned as a toddler. *Twinkle…twinkle…little star. How I wonder what you are.* Forty miles from Charity, he reached into the bag on the desk, withdrew a pair of latex gloves, then pulled them on and snapped them at the wrist.

Taking a seat, he dumped out the box of eight crayons, then put on his glasses and slid the sheet of plain white typing paper forward.

He didn't worry about forensics. Unlike those CSI shows on TV that processed evidence in nanoseconds, police labs were so busy it sometimes took weeks to get results. Not that there'd be any prints or DNA. He was hypervigilant about leaving them nothing to examine. And even if they did match fibers with the carpet or bedding in this dump, it wouldn't matter. He'd paid cash, and he'd be long gone by the time they made the match.

Resuming his humming, he composed a special note... humming and printing...humming and printing...using all of his colors...

TWINKLE, TWINKLE, DEADLY STAR
NOW IT'S TIME TO RAISE THE BAR.

With autumn on the way, night came swiftly to the thickly forested Alleghenies, dropping the temperature, cooling the air. It was eight-thirty when Margo descended her porch and hopped into Cole's truck. He smiled his approval at her long tousled hair, jeans and navy sweatshirt, then turned down the country song on the radio.

"All set?" he asked.

"All set," she repeated, fastening her seat belt. "Where are we going?"

"Someplace quiet so we can talk."

"So you've said. But I have to be able to be reached in case anything comes up."

"Got your cell phone?"

"Yes."

Cole checked his mirrors and they got under way, headlights poking through the night. "Then you can be reached. We aren't going far, and I think you'll be glad when we get there."

He was right.

Payton's Rocks was the highest point in the area, its massive boulders and rock formations nearly scraping the sky. It was one of her favorite places in the world, filled with a craggy kind of beauty and wonderful memories.

The Silverado's tires crunched over the dirt-and-gravel lot as they rolled to a stop and parked, then got out. The woods were fragrant with pines, and as always in late August, the lingering smell of blackberries sweetened the air.

Cole reached in back to grab a wide-beamed flashlight and two short-legged folding beach chairs, then he handed her the light and a stainless-steel thermos.

Margo's pulse quickened with hope. *Cocoa.* He'd brought cocoa. Did it mean something, or was it just habit?

They hadn't said much on the way. Now, flicking on the flashlight and handing it her, he nodded toward the long, narrow, wooded path leading to the rocks, and spoke quietly from behind her.

"My mom and dad called just before I came to pick you up."

Margo held her breath for a second. "How are they?" Brushy undergrowth scraped her jeans as she led the way, keeping the flashlight's beam on the uneven ground. Overhead, a thick canopy of leaves and branches kept the sky a mystery. "I hope they're doing okay."

The Blackburns hadn't handled their breakup well. His dad and brothers had had their opinions, but they'd stayed out of it. His mother was another story. Betty had phoned her, distraught, and filled with questions—suggested they speak with their minister and not rush into anything. Their talk had ended badly. That hurt almost as much as losing Cole did. Almost.

"They're doing fine."

"I'm glad." But she couldn't help wondering how the conversation had gone after he told them where he was, what he was doing and who he was doing it with. "I know I should've asked about them before, but—"

"It's okay. Some things are easier to talk about than others."

Yes, they were, she thought, recalling Cole's closed look when her mom called her cell phone the other day.

"Dad could've retired from the force last year, but he chose to stay on, so Mom's making noises about substitute teaching again."

That was a surprise. She could only think of two couples who were more traditional than the Blackburns: her parents and June and Ward Cleaver. "How's your dad handling that?"

"He's dead set against it. He says they don't need the money and this is her time to relax after raising three boys. She says she's tired of trying to fill her days while he's working. They always talked about the things they'd do after he retired. Travel, visit the grandkids, see Yellowstone. Now she says if he won't retire, she won't, either."

"Hang on." Margo flashed the light over a raised, exposed root on the path. "Watch your step."

"I see it. Anyway," he said as they moved on. "My money's on Mom."

"Then you think she'll be teaching?"

He chuckled softly. "No, I think my dad'll retire."

Smiling, Margo fell silent, wondering if she'd ever have children who talked about her and their father with such affection—and without even uttering the word *love*. How blessed Cole was to still have both of them. And how blessed Betty and Pete were to have each other. She only wished her mom and dad had had more time together. If her dad had lived...things might've worked out differently for all of them.

The path opened wide enough for them to walk side-by-side, then wider still. Margo's heart swelled as they left the trees and underbrush to stand in a dirt clearing beneath God's glorious handiwork. Straight ahead were the centuries-old rock behemoths, while overhead and beyond the rocks, the endless black sky hosted billions upon billions of twinkling stars and a thin crescent moon. She was at the top of the world...so close to Heaven she could almost touch the wings of angels.

"Glad you came now?" he asked quietly.

Margo smiled. "Yes." But that didn't tell her why he'd chosen to talk here. Her question was answered a few minutes later when their chairs were facing north on the long, raised rock plateau where they'd stargazed many times before.

They kept their voices hushed.

"This is probably the last night for the Perseid meteor shower. I wanted to check it out when it was at its peak, but the cloud cover and rain had other ideas. And as an added bonus—" he unsnapped a case on his belt and withdrew a pair of binoculars "—we should be able to see Jupiter on the southern horizon. Tonight's perfect. No light pollution, the moon's nearly dark and there's no cloud cover."

"Perfect," she replied because she had to say something. But underneath, she felt like a yo-yo, letting her hopes rise, then fall, only to rise and fall again. Despite the cocoa, this trip wasn't a prelude to finding their way back to each other. It was about efficiency—discussing the case and watching the sky at the same time. But it was so beautiful here, she couldn't allow herself to be disappointed.

Cole passed the binoculars to her. "I take it you haven't heard or read anything about the meteor shower?"

She looked through the glasses. "I try not to watch news programs or pick up the paper. Every time I do, some reporter's wondering why the Charity P.D. isn't doing its job."

"In those words?"

"No," she said, bringing down the glasses. "That's my battered self-esteem talking."

"Does your battered self-esteem have something to do with the reporter you wanted to pop earlier today?"

Margo passed the binoculars to him. "She wondered if it was time for me to step down and let someone with more experience take a crack at the case. Now I'm wondering if she's right."

He squeezed her hand. "She's not. It's only been five days, and unlike last time, he's communicating. He'll slip up. When he does, you'll get him." He opened the thermos, removed the cap and the smaller cup inside, then filled them.

"How about a toast?" he said, smiling and handing her the larger one.

"Okay. To what?" To more nights like this one, sipping cocoa and looking for shooting stars? Not likely.

Before he could speak, her cell phone chimed out a tune and she stifled a sigh at the interruption. "Give me a second." *Please,* she prayed as she took it from

her pocket. *Don't let this call take me away from here.*
Then she saw the number in the ID window, and knew
it would. She flipped open the phone.

"Steve?"

"We got him."

Adrenaline shot to every nerve and muscle in Margo's
body. "You got *him?*"

"Maybe," he returned, reading her correctly. "Chase
Merritt came back to his apartment. We'd spoken to the
neighbors across the street days ago, so they knew he
was wanted for questioning. One of them was walking
her dog in her backyard and saw a man—on foot—use
a key and let himself inside. She's pretty sure it was
Merritt."

"Pick him up," she said, standing. "I'm on my way."

Cole was on his feet now, too. "Who?" he asked, when
she'd ended the call.

Margo tucked the phone back in her pocket, deeply
regretting what she had to say—for her sake and for
Cole's. She knew how much he'd counted on watching
the skies tonight, but she had a job to do. Somewhere in
the back of her mind, it occurred to her that even though
she had just cause, in a way she was saying no to him
again.

"I am so sorry," she said, meeting his eyes in the near
dark. "It's Chase Merritt. Our BOLO boy just showed
up. I have to leave."

But Cole was already dumping their drinks and gathering their gear. "Maybe this is the break we needed.
Let's go."

TEN

Twenty minutes later, Margo sank to the corner of her desk and shook her head. "That's disappointing." Not only was Merritt gone again, she and Cole had left Payton's Rocks and all those stars for nothing. And if she were honest with herself, she was more upset about the latter, though Cole probably wasn't. His focus, as always, was clearly on the case.

"Sorry," O'Dell said in the same subdued tone. "He was gone when I got there. I drove around looking for him, since Mrs. Sheldon said he was on foot, but there was literally no one on the streets."

"Mrs. Sheldon was sure it was Merritt, not someone using his key?"

"I asked her that, too. She said she was as sure as she could be. They've been neighbors since he moved in last year, and she's seen him come and go fairly often, so... I think it was him."

"Okay," she said wearily. "Let's try questioning his friends again—see if any of them bear watching. If he's been holing up nearby, and he was on foot, he'll surface again. Check the friends who have garages first—someplace he can stash his SUV. But let's not cancel the BOLO, just in case."

O'Dell cast a cold glance at Cole, who was checking out the old posters on the walls, then ambled closer to Margo and lowered his voice. "Here's a thought. Maybe you and I should stake out the guy's place in case he comes back. You up for it?"

Margo considered that as she reached for the Pepsi she'd taken from her stash in the department's small refrigerator, then popped the tab. "Not a bad idea, but chances are Merritt got what he needed and won't be back tonight. Brett's coming in at eleven. He can drive by a few times to check for activity there. Besides, you've been on since two, and you have to be back here at eight in the morning. You need to get some sleep."

"How about tomorrow night?" he said, softening his voice even more. "I could change shifts with Charlie."

An uneasy feeling crept up Margo's back. "No, Charlie needs to work days. He's driving his daughter to her sonogram at three. With her due date so close and her husband still in Afghanistan, he wants to be there for her. We'll figure something out."

"Right," he said, with another cold glance at Cole. Then, crossing to the coffeemaker, he filled his mug and went to the other desk in the room to start some paperwork.

Margo stilled. What was going on here? When John was alive, they'd partnered often, and Steve had always treated her like a colleague, nothing more. Now this. Was he interested in her? Or was he irritated because he felt Cole was infringing on his territory? Mentally tossing up her hands, she put her Pepsi down and walked over to Cole.

"You should go," she said quietly. "I need to stick around here for a while."

Cole glanced at Steve's sullen expression, then nodded.

"What about your car? I can run you home for it, or come back and get you when you're finished here."

"Thanks, but I'll take one of the cruisers home, or Steve can drop me off when Brett comes in." She lowered her voice. "Thanks for the trip to the rocks. And the cocoa."

His dark eyes warmed. "Even though you didn't have a chance to taste it?"

"Even though. For as long as it lasted, it was the best part of my day."

"Mine, too." He continued to hold her gaze, and Margo felt that undeniable pull to step into his arms again. Step into his life again.

From across the room, O'Dell cleared his throat.

Cole frowned. "Okay, I'm gone. I want to be at the school first thing in the morning. If I learn anything promising, we can talk about it over lunch. If you want."

Oh, yes, she wanted, but plans had a way of changing these days. "Sounds good, but let's leave it open, okay?"

"Okay." He started to go, then grinned and came back to her. "By the way, I hope you noticed that I didn't tell you to be careful even once today."

She had to smile. "Good night. See you tomorrow."

Margo glanced at the clock on the station wall, pushed her paperwork and cold breakfast biscuit aside, then picked up the phone and tapped in a number—the first of three calls she needed to make this morning.

Steve had taken her home last night, but only remembered then that Adam Wilcox had phoned earlier. Unfortunately, it had been too late to return his call then, and too early to contact him when she had come in this morning. It was now eight-thirty. She hoped Adam was up and about.

The phone continued to ring. Six rings...seven... eight... Then the answering machine clicked on, and Margo's heart constricted with sympathy when John Wilcox's voice said he couldn't come to the phone right now, but he'd get back to her as soon he could.

She waited for the beep, then left a message. "Adam, it's Margo. Sorry I didn't get back to you last night, but it was late when I learned that you'd called. Call me here at the station, or on my cell phone. You have the number."

She broke the connection. Now she needed to nag the PSP again before she contacted Grayson Security about an alarm system. The other phone rang. Margo let Sarah answer it, hoping it wasn't another call from the media. But when the redheaded dispatcher turned around, her pudgy face was lined. Grabbing the TV's remote control from her desk, she turned down the volume on *It's a Good Day, America.*

"Margo, Ollie Murdock over at the newspaper's on line two. He sounds anxious."

Margo picked up. "Ollie? It's Margo. What's wrong?"

"I think your killer's getting hungry for more press. Dorothy just brought in a letter that was placed in the night-delivery slot sometime last night after eleven. I was here from six to eleven getting a jump on my editorial, so I'm certain of the time. The box was empty when I left. You better take a look at this."

"I'll be right over," she said, already on her feet. "Don't let anyone else touch it."

Minutes later, she was in Ollie's office and staring at a crayoned message that struck fear into her heart.

Now it's time to raise the bar? Dear God. What did that mean? More killings? The killing of an important person? Margo slipped on latex gloves, picked up the sheet and envelope, then placed them in an evidence bag. Her pulse was pounding so hard in her ears she could barely hear herself speak.

"Thanks, Ollie. Please. I know this is asking a lot, but could you sit on this for a day? Maybe two? I promise that when this is all over, I'll give you an exclusive. Just give us some time to figure out what this means and take steps to prevent whatever's next on his agenda."

Frowning, Ollie wiped his hand back over his bald head as if smoothing nonexistent hairs. "You ready to say this guy's local?"

"Not yet." Because she just didn't know and it was eating her up inside. She snapped off her gloves. "I'll get back to you as soon as I can." He hadn't said he'd sit on the story, but without a refusal, she had to believe he'd comply. Striding outside to her black-and-white, she pulled out her cell phone.

"Sarah?" she said when the dispatcher answered. "Get the department together for a meeting in a half hour."

"Will do. Brett probably just got to bed, but I'll wake him up. How about Cole?"

"He's at the high school." She checked her watch. "In fact he probably just arrived. I'll call him on my way." Checking those yearbooks would have to wait. "See you in a few minutes."

Margo, Steve, Fish, Charlie and Brett sat together at the table in the small, rarely used interrogation room, staring at the colorful note Ollie had received. Across from her, Cole leaned against the wood-paneled wall, dressed in faded jeans, boots and a black polo shirt.

Even now with her nerves thrumming and new evidence to examine, she was acutely aware of him. In the open doorway, Sarah waited expectantly, watching the front door and listening for calls.

"Okay," Margo said gravely. "I made a call to the Burgess and Tate carnival's home base when I got back from the paper. Ray Masters is off the hook. He was already gone when this note showed up at the newspaper. The manager vouched for him. That means we're ninety-percent sure we're dealing with someone local. It's possible that Chase Merritt's back in town, and that shines a light on him. But we know he was on a tour of duty when the original murders occurred, so—copycatting aside— he might only be able to help by supplying information on other men who were interested in Leanne Hudson." She paused. "Back to the note. Any thoughts? What does he mean by, 'Now it's time to raise the bar'?"

Steve O'Dell replied first. "Don't misunderstand what I'm about to say. I'm not making less of the murders he's committed. But if he was only going to kill another woman, why announce it, and why hint that his next act or next victim would be more important?"

Fish chimed in, a reluctant message in his eyes. "Someone important enough for Ollie to put him on the front page again. Someone like the mayor...or another woman who has some power in this town."

Margo tried to ignore the inference, but he did have a point. She glanced at Sarah, still standing sentinel in the doorway. "Sarah, we need to call Bernice when we're though here, okay?"

"Okay."

"There's another possibility," Brett put in. "Is he hinting that more than one woman would be killed on the same night—or that there would be murders on consecutive nights? Maybe this is about numbers or time."

"Anyone else?" Margo asked, her gaze locking on Cole's.

It was easy to read the grim concern in his dark eyes. He and Fish were on the same page. He was thinking that she'd already been warned, and taking out a cop was a killer's badge of honor. That would definitely raise the bar. She'd thought of that, too, even before Fish's statement. And her stomach wasn't handling it well.

He pushed away from the wall. "When the first murders occurred, Margo and I did some research on the basic similarities among serial killers. I've also spoken to detectives in Manhattan who've dealt with this sort of thing. Usually, serial killers don't change the way they do business, or change their signatures. They continue to do what feels comfortable—what fills their need. But sometimes they evolve. Maybe this killer's so new to the game, he's still trying to figure out what kind of monster he wants to be."

O'Dell pinned Cole with a look. "He's not that new. If he's numbering his victims with stars, he's already up to four."

"I did say 'maybe.' We're just throwing out ideas here, right?" He paused. "The other thing is, I think Margo mentioned that there could be a tie-in to school days since he's using crayons and stars."

Charlie repositioned himself at the table, his chair scraping on the tile floor. "You think that school starting next week might've triggered the latest murder?"

"It could have. That brings us back to the old questions. Why did he take a two-year hiatus between killings? Did he leave and return? Was he sick and unable? We know that three of the murders occurred in August. What's special about this month? Or is it just a coincidence?"

Her stomach wasn't getting any better. Margo stepped in. "Okay, except for Steve and Cole, we all grew up here, which means we know the troublemakers. We might've picked him up before. Let's go through our files again. Thankfully, we're a small community. We don't have hundreds of them."

There was a spattering of agreement at the table.

"Okay," she said, exhaling. "Same as before. We're looking for white males between eighteen and thirty-two, except this time let's pay close attention to men who went to school here. He's organized. That might show up in our files as someone with higher education."

"He could also be a dropout who watches a lot of TV," Steve countered. "Seems like every crime drama on the tube these days teaches killers how not to get caught."

"True enough, but let's stick with the statistics for now—keeping in mind that the profile's just a guideline." Margo handed the plastic evidence bag to Fish. "Photograph it, then take it to the PSP for prints and fiber analysis. Remind them that this is their case, too. Tell them we can't afford to take a number anymore."

She turned to Brett. "Go home and get some sleep. When you come back—"

"Margo!" Sarah gasped from the doorway. "That Talbot woman's on TV. She says she got a phone call that could've come from the killer."

Everyone scrambled out of the room and gathered near the set. Sarah turned up the sound. They were too late to get more than Talbot's steely-eyed teaser: "Was it a prank? Or did I actually speak with the killer? Stay tuned for Channel 29 News at Noon."

"Sarah," Margo said coldly. "Get me Channel 29's station manager on the phone, please."

By the time Margo unlocked the door to her home at four-thirty, her nerve endings were stretched to the breaking point and her sadness was profound. The media had swarmed like ground bees, all the radio and TV stations in the area and beyond clamoring for information after Nancy Talbot's ridiculous teaser. Her anonymous call *had* turned out to be a tasteless teenage prank, and the station had known that before the teaser aired. But it was enough to start the phones ringing off the hook, even though everyone at the station had so much work to do.

Combing the files had produced a handful of possible suspects. Cole and an officer from the PSP were checking them out. And, as expected, there'd been no prints on Ollie's note. In the middle of everything, Adam had returned her call and asked if they could get together. He was down and he needed to talk, and it hurt her more than she could say to put him off until tomorrow afternoon. He assured her that he understood, though, and said he'd see her soon. But that didn't make her feel any better.

Feeling utterly beaten, Margo stepped inside, locked the kitchen door behind her…and let the tears come.

Now it's time to raise the bar.

Sinking to a chair, she hugged the fear in her stomach. The PSP was now taking a more active role, so she had help. But would it be enough? Heaven only knew. She was terrified that someone else's daughter would die unless they got a break soon. And it would be her fault because she wasn't a good enough cop to stop it.

You're overreacting, a tiny voice chided from the back of her mind. That's exhaustion talking.

Maybe it was, but the ache in her heart was real and distracting and right now, she believed Nancy Talbot's claim that she wasn't the person for the job.

Worn-out and so tired of playing the tough cop, she turned to the One she'd turned her back on a year go. The only One who could change things for the better.

"Help me," she whispered through her tears. "I can't do this by myself. I've tried, and I can't do it. But You have the power to stop this terrible man. I came to You before, asking for my dad's life, asking for Cole's love." Her voice caught, and she swallowed.

"I'm not asking for myself this time. I'm asking for the town and for the next victim. I swear, if You help me end this, I'll…" Her spirits sank even further. What could she offer God that He couldn't have for Himself anytime He chose?

Someone knocked at the front door.

Margo sprang up and wiped her face.

The knock came again.

Grabbing a paper towel from the dispenser, she wiped her eyes again, blew her nose and cleared her throat. Then she dropped the paper towel in the wastebasket and hurried to open the door.

When she saw him standing there, she broke down again.

Cole didn't say a word. He came inside, closed the door and let the compassion in his eyes and his strong arms do his talking for him.

For a few moments, he simply held her, rocking her gently as she clung to him. Then, pulling herself together but unwilling to move from the comfort of his arms, Margo tipped her gaze up to his and swallowed.

"Oh, Cole, I'm so afraid he'll hurt someone else, and it'll be on my head."

"I know," he returned quietly. "But it's not your fault that leads go nowhere and the evidence isn't panning out. You've warned women to be cautious. For now, you've done what you can."

"But it's not enough."

"That's why we're both going to pray hard and keep on praying until this is resolved. Right?"

She nodded.

"Good."

He held her face, kissed her forehead, kissed her nose...kissed her lips. And new tears threatened to come.

"You taste salty," he murmured with a smile. "Know what's great after something salty?"

She shook her head.

"Ice cream. Let's drive down to the valley and get a couple of cones at Rachel's place. You can even have chocolate sprinkles on yours. Didn't you tell me once that chocolate jump-starts the feel-good hormones in our brains?"

"I can't. I'm going back out in a little while."

Disapproval wiped the smile from his face. "I know. Charlie told me, and we both thought it was a lousy idea. But you're the boss, and I made you a promise, so I'm not going to harp on the subject. I'll have you back in plenty of time to stake out Merritt's place. So say yes."

Margo looked at him through watery eyes. She couldn't handle the guilt of going. "If I go out for ice cream in the middle of this mess and someone sees me, I'll be tarred and feathered."

"Stop. I know how you feel, but you don't have to wear a hair shirt. I repeat, the only thing you—*we*—can do right now is follow the evidence and stay aware. You and the guys have questioned over a hundred people in the past six days. You're in constant touch with the state police. You're doing what you can. Now, please. Splash some cold water on your face, change to street clothes and let's go. I'll even spring for a hot dog if you want one."

She sent him a wobbly smile. How could she love him more at this moment than she had at any other? And how terribly sad that a love this strong wasn't returned.

"Thank you," she whispered, pulling the hairpins out of her soft bun. "I'd love to have ice cream with you. I'll be back in a minute."

"Thank You, Lord," Margo murmured as she changed clothes and tucked her cell phone in her jeans pocket. "You keep sending him to me just when I need him the most. I'm not sure what that means—and I won't ask. But thank You."

Patterson's Campground and Cabins was a hub of activity when Margo and Cole left his truck and walked across the pine-shaded, winding dirt driveway to the camp store. It was a happy place, the ding-ping-ding of arcade games carrying to them over the upbeat music inside. Set on fifty acres of forestland, with trees and undergrowth separating the cabins and tent sites, it was a veritable haven for the hundreds of city dwellers Rachel usually hosted in the summer months. She had it all here. A shallow creek kept little ones happily splashing and searching for crayfish, and there was a crystal-blue pool behind the store for swimming and sunbathing. Shuffle-board, organized games and karaoke, too.

Rachel beamed when the two of them entered the well-stocked store together and walked up to the small dairy bar. "Let me guess. One small vanilla cone with chocolate sprinkles, and a large chocolate cone, without. Then you're going to drive around and look for elk."

Cole grinned. "Hi, Rachel. No, we're just here for ice cream—and a couple of hot dogs. Margo has to work tonight, but I talked her into a short break from the lunacy in town."

Rachel frowned wryly. "Good idea." She looked at Margo. "The statement you gave the local TV and radio stations played a few times this afternoon. Will the reporter be charged?"

"Unfortunately, no, because there actually was a call, and she did say it could've been a prank. The kids who made the call will probably get something out of it, though."

That fire was out, but there was another one smoldering. Now she had to hope that Ollie would honor her request and keep the latest note under wraps for a while.

"Okay, enough shoptalk," Rachel said, changing the subject. "First things first. You need hot dogs, and if I recall correctly, you like them burned a bit. What would you like on them?"

Twenty minutes later they strolled the shaded lane that wound through the campground. It was quiet this far back from the store and pool, though some sound did carry. The distant laughter of children...the occasional birdsong...their gritty footfalls on the path.

"She's got her hands full here," Cole said, cutting his chocolate cone down to size. "Even with a small staff. But she seems to be handling it okay."

"She seems to be. But no one knows what goes on when she's alone. Jack's death really took its toll." Jack

Patterson had died cutting timber just before Christmas two years ago, ending one of the most loving relationships Margo had ever witnessed. "I didn't expect her to reopen the business after he passed away."

Cole's mood sobered. "People do what they have to after a loss. They dig in their heels, deal with it and make the best of what they have left. It's like the Serenity Prayer that's hanging in your mom's kitchen. They accept the things they can't change."

When he looked away and turned his attention to his ice cream again, his grave expression told her he wasn't talking only about Rachel's loss. He was talking about theirs, too.

Margo let the silence between them stretch on as they walked for a few minutes, then gathered her courage and spoke quietly. "Are you happy, Cole?"

He glanced at her again, but only briefly. "Happy about what?"

"Happy with your life. Happy with your profession. It's been eleven months since we—" She couldn't finish the sentence. "What I mean is, I want you to be happy. I never meant to hurt you."

He released a sigh. "We hurt each other, Margo. But things are better now. We're friends again. Right?"

There was that F-word again, and it hurt just as much this time. But once more, if friendship was the only thing he was willing to offer, she'd take what she could get. "Yes. We're friends."

"Good. Now, can I ask my friend a question without her going ballistic on me?"

She had to smile. "Yes, you can."

"Charlie said you're staking out Merritt's place alone tonight. Let me ride shotgun." A nerve leaped in his jaw when she shook her head. "Why not?"

"Because I just said no to someone else, and if I say yes to you, there's going to be trouble. Believe me, I'd welcome the company. But I can't ask you to come along."

When she'd spoken with O'Dell last night, his resentment had been easy to see—and Cole's inclusion in the case seemed to be the reason for it. He hadn't confirmed it, but if she'd guessed correctly, there was no point in making things worse. When Cole went back to Pittsburgh, she and Steve would still have to work together.

He seemed to know who she was talking about. "You're sure it'll cause problems?"

"Yes. If you were there at my invitation."

Curiosity creased his features as he seemed to examine her words and realize she'd left an option on the table. He stopped walking and met her eyes. "What if I just happened by?"

"What you do in the evening is your own business."

"Let me get this straight. You're saying it's now okay for me to hang around and watch your back—without having my head handed to me?"

Nodding, she started walking again.

He fell into step beside her. "Mind if I ask what changed your mind?"

"Something you said a few days ago," she replied. "I'd like to think I'm smarter than those heroines in gothic films who carry candles up to the attic to check for creepy noises." She sighed then. "But for the next few minutes, can we just walk and enjoy our cones, and pretend that the whole world is a safe and beautiful place?"

"Sure. As soon as you tell me why you turned down the other guy's offer."

Tell him, that tiny voice at the back of her mind prodded. Tell him you refused Steve because you hoped that *he* would make the same offer. Tell him you love him and want to spend as much time with him as you can before he leaves you again.

No way.

"Because everyone in the department's been working overtime since this whole Gold Star thing began, and they're getting burned-out. They need their evenings off when they can get them. I couldn't let him give up the only one he's had in days."

She kicked a stone with the toe of her sneaker, then met his eyes again. "And," she said. "I think you're a better cop than he is. I trust you."

A lovely warmth enveloped her when Cole replied with a quiet smile, "I trust you, too. *Now* the world's a safe and beautiful place."

ELEVEN

Locust Street started out long and flat, then rose to a steep hill before turning right and merging with the state route. Chase Merritt lived midway up Locust.

Margo sat in her mother's dark blue Ford Escort with the driver's side window down, sipping strong coffee and listening to the night sounds. Most of the town was asleep, but she could still hear the occasional hum of tires down on Sassafras Street and the low buzz from a sodium-vapor streetlight about to shine its last. Cole was parked on the opposite side of the street facing her, halfway up the rise.

Margo's cell phone chimed softly, and smiling, she pulled it from the pocket of her black windbreaker. He'd been calling her every ten or fifteen minutes since they'd set up at ten o'clock. It was now twenty-seven minutes past midnight.

"You still awake?"

She loved the low warm timbre of his voice, loved speaking in quiet tones in the darkness. Clichéd as it sounded, they could've been the only two people left in the world. At least the only two people on this street who were awake. Except for the occasional electric candle in a window, the houses were dark.

"How can I sleep when you're constantly calling me?"

He chuckled softly. "I've got another riddle for you."

"Oh, please," she groaned. "I haven't figured out the last one yet."

"Quit whining and listen closely. This is an easy one."

"Okay, I'm listening."

"A man leaves home, makes three left turns, and on his way home he sees two men wearing masks. Where is he?"

"That doesn't make any sense."

"Sure it does. It took my eight-year-old niece five minutes to figure it out. Call me with your answer. The clock's ticking."

Margo closed her phone, sank back against the headrest and pursed her lips. *A man leaves home...makes three left turns...* She opened her phone and hit the redial button.

Cole chuckled. "That was quick. Where is he?"

"I don't know yet. Is he driving a police cruis—" A jolt of adrenaline stopped her in midsentence. At the same moment, a dog started to bark. "Cole, someone's coming through the backyard between Merritt's place and the neighbor on the left. Can you see him?"

Tension entered his voice. "No. Not from this angle."

Margo raised night-vision binoculars to her eyes. "He's behind that big lilac bush near the corner of the house now. I don't know if he's just— Okay, he's heading for the back porch. I think it's him."

"I'm on my way. Wait for me."

"See you in back of Merritt's place."

Margo tossed the binoculars on the seat, jammed her phone back in her pocket and opened the door. Without a bulb, the interior of the car stayed dark.

She closed the door softly, then started walking, head down, unsnapping the holster hidden beneath her windbreaker. She could see Cole coming toward her at the same not-quite-hurried pace. Cutting through the adjacent yards, they met at the back of Merritt's place and crept up to the porch…peered through the kitchen window. The only light came from the open refrigerator door. Big, muscle-bound Chase Merritt was hungry.

Margo nodded and drew her gun. Cole did the same.

She gave three loud raps at the door, then flattened herself against the house's siding. "Open up! Charity P.D.!"

The light went out. Rapid footfalls echoed inside the house.

Cole leaped over the low railing on the left and raced toward the front; Margo took three short steps to the right and bolted toward the street.

They reached the front just as Merritt burst through the front door and vaulted down the steps. With a running leap, Cole knocked him to the sidewalk in an all-out tackle and pinned him to the ground. He pulled his Smith & Wesson from the back of his jeans. And Merritt stopped struggling.

"Nice work," Margo said, standing over the two of them.

"Thanks," he said, glancing up and breathing hard. "I thought so."

She kept her gun drawn until he'd applied handcuffs, then holstered it and smiled down at their angry prisoner.

"Good evening, Mr. Merritt. As you've probably

guessed, we'd like to talk to you. But of course," she added, her voice cooling, "you have the right to remain silent...."

Chase Merritt stared at her from across the table in the interrogation room. He was nearly as tall as Cole, but with an extra twenty pounds on his shoulders and biceps. His salon-cut brown hair, trimmed beard and gold ear studs said he spent some time in front of a mirror. He wouldn't like the slowly bruising scrape on his cheek, compliments of the concrete walk.

"Let's get on with it, okay?" he said.

Margo leaned back in her chair to assess him. "You're sure you don't want a lawyer?"

"I'm sure." He glanced at Cole, who stood near the door. "I can talk to you two a lot cheaper on my own. So here's my statement. When I heard she was dead, I ran. I knew you'd blame me, especially if you talked to Ellie. Which, obviously, you did." His gaze ricocheted coldly between the two of them. "Well, I got a news flash—for you *and* her. I didn't do it. Now if you'll take off the cuffs, I'd like to go home."

Margo frowned, disgusted that this man who'd supposedly cared about Leanne Hudson showed no remorse over her death. "Sorry, we're just getting started. Let's talk about where you've been staying for the past week, then we'll move on. If you didn't hurt the Hudson girl and you were keeping close tabs on her, you might know who did. I'm going to need a list."

An hour later, after Merritt had been processed and taken to a cell, Margo said goodbye to Brett, left a note for Sarah saying she'd be in late tomorrow, then headed for the door. There was a good chance that Merritt's alibi for the murder would check out, but that information wouldn't clear for several hours. Not until they could contact the woman he'd been with. Until then, he was their guest. As for her hope that Merritt could name other men he'd seen Leanne with, the best he could come up with were the college guys on her volleyball team, and they'd already checked out.

Leaving the station, Margo took the short driveway to the department's small side lot where her mom's Escort was parked beside the building. The town was deadly quiet, the moonless night and cloud cover deepening the shadows despite the saffron glow of the streetlights.

She kept her eyes moving as she pulled her keys from her windbreaker. She wasn't afraid. But as she'd told Bernice Marshall when she'd phoned her, caution and a healthy respect for the unknown were now the order of the day.

She was about to climb into the Escort when she spotted a black truck in the shadows beyond one of the cruisers. Cole was slouched in his seat and dozing, his open window letting in the cooler night air.

Smiling, Margo walked toward him. His eyes flew open when she reached his open window.

"I thought I told you to go home," she said.

He squeezed his eyes shut, then opened them again—rubbed his face. "Back to Pittsburgh?"

"No, back to Jenna's. What are you doing out here?"

Straightening, he rolled his shoulders, working out the stiffness. "Waiting for you. I'll follow you home before I head up the hill." He pulled on his headlights. "Do you want to switch cars?"

"No, I'll keep Mom's for now. I'll ask one of the guys to follow me over to her place tomorrow." She softened her voice. "Cole, thank you. For everything."

"You're welcome. For everything."

Then she strode back to the Escort, more confused about their relationship than ever.

On Tuesday morning at ten-thirty when Margo walked into the station, she felt better spiritually than she had in months. More accepting. Last night, feeling overwhelmed by the case and her relationship with Cole, and needing solace, she'd opened her book of scriptures. Something wonderful had happened. As she'd reread some of her favorite passages, she'd felt her heart soften. Felt some inner peace return. She'd always loved the psalms, and the comforting words of Psalm 107:1 still lived in her mind. "Give thanks to the Lord for He is good; His love endures forever."

Sarah handed her a cup of coffee and flashed a handful of pink notes. "Looks like those kids on the west end of town had a lot of fun last night. You'd think there was a full moon."

"What happened?"

"They damaged four mailboxes, raided half a dozen gardens and spray-painted smiley faces on the signs in Elmer Fox's front yard. He's in a real snit this morning. They got his garden, too. He says they took his three biggest cantaloupes."

"Wonderful. Did he recognize the kids?"

"No, he didn't even see them. But he's sure it was Mookie Miller and his four-wheeler bunch. He said the four of them were racing around, tearing up one of the fields near his house earlier last night. Elmer brought in the paint cans they left in his yard. He wants them fingerprinted, and he wants his cantaloupes back."

Margo shook her head. "Those kids need to get back to school."

"There's more. Ben Caruthers over at the hardware store called, too. Last night, someone swiped a wheelbarrow from out front of his place. I keep telling him that we don't live in Mayberry and that he needs to take his stuff in at night. Know what he says to that?"

"That if you trust people, they'll be trustworthy?"

She nodded. "I think he's singing a different tune this morning. Fish went over to see him. That was around eight."

"Good," Margo said, carrying her coffee back to her desk. "What are we doing about the vandalism?"

Sarah's swivel chair squeaked as she spun around. "Fish is at the Miller farm now talking to Mookie since he's the ringleader. He's going to tell him that we fingerprinted the paint cans and see how the kid reacts."

"Okay." She knew how that would go. Fish would get a confession, and Mookie and his three cousins would be doing community service again. She'd make sure every garden they hit was weed free for the rest of the season. The folks at the senior center wouldn't be washing their own dishes for a while, either. "How's our prisoner doing?"

Sarah shrugged. "I don't know. I don't go back there. All I know is, he complained about his breakfast, and Fish says his alibi checked out."

"Well, then," Margo said wryly, putting her coffee down and heading for the cells. "I guess we should spring him." After that, she would definitely call Grayson Security.

It was nearly 7:00 p.m. when Margo parked her red Cherokee in the diner's lot and strode up the walk toward Adam, who was waiting outside the restaurant. Grayson Security had finally gotten back to her just before

5:00 p.m. They were currently installing all the security
bells and whistles in a bank that was nearly ready to
open, and would be unable to start work on her house
until Monday morning. Sarah, who'd overheard the call,
had fretted over the delay, and reminded her that Cole
wouldn't like it, either. But until then, her motion lights,
steel doors—and more importantly, her Glock—would
do just fine.

She approached Adam just as he said thanks to a
woman and her two friends, one of whom squeezed his
hand before she entered the diner.

"Hi," Margo said, giving him a brief hug. "I'm so
sorry I had to postpone our meeting again. Have you
been waiting long?"

"No, I just got here a minute ago." He sent her a weak
smile. "And to be honest, now that I'm here, I'm not sure
I want to go inside."

Margo searched his face. "Is something wrong?"

"It's a little too busy in there."

"Are you afraid we won't find a seat?"

He slipped his hands in the pockets of the long
navy shorts he wore with a blue-and-gray Penn State
sweatshirt. The sleeves were torn off above his biceps.
"No, I'm sure there's room." The blue eyes beneath his
blond-streaked surfer hair were too bleak for someone so
young. "I've been sticking real close to the house since
the funeral. I still have a hard time talking when people
ask how I'm doing." He nodded toward the restaurant's
door. "Like Mrs. Winslow."

Margo felt a sympathetic tug. He was afraid of tearing
up and embarrassing himself. "I had the same trouble
when my dad passed away, but people really do mean
well. And honest emotion is nothing to be ashamed of."
She glanced through the diner's plate-glass window. It

wasn't a mob scene in there, but if he was uneasy they could leave. "Would you feel more comfortable talking at my house? Or yours?"

"No, we don't have to do that." He nodded toward the takeout window to the left of the dining room. During the summer months, Aggie did a booming ice-cream business through that window. "Maybe we could just grab something to drink and take a walk? My treat."

"I'd like that, but I really don't need anything. You go ahead. I'll wait here for you."

When Adam came back a few minutes later, he was poking a straw through the plastic lid on his milk shake. He tipped it her way. "It's peanut butter. Want to try it?"

"Thanks, but no. Where are we headed?"

Pulling on his straw, he canted his head across the street toward a tree-lined residential district. In the distance, on a diagonal offshoot of Sassafras Street, a stand of mixed trees and a stone pillar marked the side entrance to Woodland Park.

"Wait," he said. "That's probably too weird. You've been dealing with that stuff for days. Maybe we should head in the other direction."

The crime scene flashed through Margo's mind, the printed silk scarf, the water fountain, the empty-eyed stare of another young woman. She hadn't been back there since last Wednesday. Brett had removed the yellow crime-scene tape, but the memories remained.

"No," she said finally. "It's not too weird, it's just sad. It's also a beautiful park, and it should be used. Let's go."

They crossed the street, then walked toward that stone pillar, keeping their voices low as they passed people doing outside work and three little girls playing hopscotch on the colorfully chalked sidewalk.

"So what's going on?" Margo asked. "Are you okay?"

Adam shrugged. "I have to be. The loneliness is kicking in, though."

Margo didn't doubt that, especially if he'd been holed up in the house since the funeral. "Have you given any more thought to going back to school?"

"Thought about it. I told you that there's a girl there. She calls all the time asking the same thing."

"What do you tell her?"

"That I don't know. Some days I think I want to go back, sometimes I don't. Steve said it would just take time."

Margo's interest sharpened. "Steve?"

"Steve O'Dell. He came by the other day to say hello and ask if I needed anything." He smiled a little but it never reached his eyes. "He brought me a pizza. Charlie called a few times, too."

A flood of guilt washed through her. Charlie and Steve had checked on Adam, but until today, she hadn't, and she'd known him since he was a little boy. She had to do better than that.

"Steve doesn't like Cole much, does he?" Adam asked.

Steve had talked to Adam about Cole? "I'm not sure what you mean. What did he say?"

"I asked him how the Gold Star case was going, and he got kind of sarcastic. He said you guys had an ex-Manhattan cop on the job now. Said it was only a matter of time before the killer was caught and Cole was smiling from the front page of *The Sentinel*."

She didn't know what to say, so she said nothing.

Adam sampled his milk shake again. "You probably already know that I don't like him much, either."

"Why, Adam?"

"Because he tried to make my dad look bad."

"That's not true. They just had a difference of opinion."

"Dad was a fair man, Margo. It had to be more than a difference of opinion or he wouldn't have fired him. Now Cole wants to be the big man who solves the case."

Funny how death elevated loved ones to heroes on pedestals, all the mistakes they'd made in life forgotten. But there was nothing to be gained by telling Adam that his father had been wrong. "No, Cole wants to help us because he doesn't want another girl to lose her life."

"Yeah, well, that's not going to happen. It's all over. He's smart. He's moved on."

Margo sent him a puzzled look. "Why do you think that?"

"The carnival left on Sunday, and Ray Masters went with it. You'll never get him now." He looked at her. "But then, you still don't believe he's the one who killed those girls, do you?"

Margo had to bite her tongue. Obviously, O'Dell had been running his mouth about more than his dislike of Cole, and he knew better. If he didn't, he soon would. Adam was John's son, but that didn't make him privy to confidential information.

Adam stopped suddenly. Woodland Park was dead ahead, sitting in the Y between Sassafras and Teaberry Streets, the spiky black wrought-iron fencing around it suddenly making Margo think of prisons. Shaking off the thought, she focused on the primrose bushes and the tumble of tiny pink-and-white blooms poking through the fence. Shaded by broadleaf maples, ornate benches flanked the outside entrance.

"Let's just grab a bench and finish talking," Adam said, glancing over at her. "You don't really want to go in there. And it's just another reminder to me that if my dad was here, he'd be handling—" He stopped, then apologized. "I'm sorry. I didn't mean anything by that."

"It's okay," she returned. "I wish your dad was still here, too." If he was, she wouldn't be in the hot seat. "A bench is fine."

"Good. Because I need some advice, and I don't want either of us to be distracted."

When they were seated, he clasped his hands between the spread of his legs and clicked his thumbnails together. "My aunt and uncle are pressuring me to sell the house and move to Ohio with them. They say I'll never make it on my own." He sent her a trapped look. "They might be right. I hate being alone. So I've been thinking.... I do have another option. If I'm old enough to own a home, then I'm old enough to get married, right?"

Deeply troubled, but glad for coincidences, Cole finished filling his gas tank, returned the nozzle to the pump and screwed in his gas cap. Across the Quick Stop's blacktop parking lot, Steve O'Dell had just left his black-and-white and gone inside the store. Cole moved his truck to a parking space, then walked over to the police cruiser and waited. He'd already spoken to Fish Troutman—told him to spread the word. But when an opportunity presented itself, a smart man took it.

A few minutes later, O'Dell came out, peeling the strip from a package of gum. He slowed his stride when he saw Cole, then resumed the same swaggering pace. The redheaded patrolman didn't look happy to see him.

"Got a minute?" Cole said.

"Sure. What's up?"

Cole lowered his voice as the distance between them disappeared. "I have to leave for a couple of days. I need to know Margo will be safe."

O'Dell removed his dark sunglasses. The eyes beneath his thick red brows weren't kind. "You think you're the only person who watches her back?"

"No. I'm just asking the department to be a little more hands-on while I'm gone. Fish said he'd increase his drive-bys and make himself visible when he wasn't on duty. I'm hoping you'll do the same."

"Is that it?"

"No. As long as we're talking, where's all the animosity coming from? You don't like me, and that's okay. But there has to be a reason. Are you interested in Margo?"

"That's my business," O'Dell replied, a warning in his blue eyes. "But as you said, as long as we're talking... When you left the department, I took your place. I don't plan on the position being temporary."

Cole nodded. "All right, if this is about turf wars, we don't have a problem. I'm only here because this case cost me. When it's resolved I'm gone."

O'Dell narrowed his eyes. "You came back here because you lost your job over this case? This is some kind of vendetta with you?"

No, he'd come back because he'd lost his *life* over this case. His job, Margo...the home he'd been breaking his back to finish. "Yeah," he finally answered. "In a way." He extended his hand. "Are we good now?"

O'Dell didn't smile and he didn't say the rift between them was over, but he accepted Cole's handshake. "I'll keep a close eye on Margo. We all will." He put his glasses back on, though the sun was setting and the necessity for them was waning. Then Cole realized they were prescription lenses.

"I just have one more question."

Cole nodded for him to go ahead.

"If you're not sticking around, and there's nothing between you and Margo anymore, why do you give a donkey's hind leg what happens to her?"

The question jabbed at old wounds. He didn't *want* to care this much. In fact, he was diligently trying not to. Because if he let himself care any more, the day they went their separate ways, he'd be walking around with another hole in his belly.

"We were engaged." It was all he was willing to tell a stranger, and more than he was willing to tell himself.

O'Dell rolled a stick of gum and stuck it in his mouth, his features still far from friendly. "See you when you get back."

"See you," Cole repeated. A minute later, he was in his truck, listening to Margo's cell phone ring. She finally picked up.

"Hi. I hope I didn't get you at a bad time."

"Not at all," she said, but he heard a low note in her voice. "I was just getting into my car."

"You sound down. What's going on?"

"I was just out walking with Adam. He's trying to decide whether to stay here, or sell the house and move to Ohio with his aunt and uncle. He doesn't want to leave. But his aunt keeps telling him that he's too young to accept so much responsibility. She wants him with her."

"How does he feel about that?"

"How would you feel about giving up your home, especially so soon after losing someone you loved? How does anyone handle two such difficult losses so close together?"

One day at a time and with a lot of help from God, he thought, seeing the parallel to his own life. That's the only way anyone *can* handle it. "What did you tell him?"

"The same thing that Steve and Charlie told him— that now wasn't the time for him to be making big decisions. Especially when he told me he was looking at other options. Cole, you're not going to believe this. He's thinking about asking his girl to marry him so he won't have to live alone."

"Whoa," he replied, startled. "Is he serious?"

"I don't know. I hope I talked him out of it. I asked him to please call me before he makes any rash moves. He doesn't even call her by name. He refers to her as 'a girl at school.' I'm really afraid he's going to do something he'll regret."

"Well, if he thinks marriage is the solution to his loneliness, his aunt and uncle have a valid argument for him dumping the house and moving to Ohio."

"I told him I thought he needed grief counseling and offered to set up an appointment for him with Reverend Landers's group, but he...I don't know. I think I hit a nerve, because he got defensive."

"Some people don't like opening up to strangers."

"Apparently, he's one of them." She changed the subject. "Tell me about your day. What have you been up to?"

Nothing he wanted to do, that was for sure. "Packing. That's why I called. I have to drag out my surveillance equipment and go to work for a few days. If I don't, I won't have a job to go back to."

"Oh," she said quietly.

"Yeah. Oh." Neither of them said anything for a few seconds, then Margo spoke again. "Well...stay safe. I hope the days are productive."

"Same here. I need to wrap this one up and focus on a project that makes me feel good." He'd been referring to his upcoming case, but once again, his partially constructed home came to mind. Every piece of Sheetrock he nailed to the studs made it look and feel more like a real home—gave him a warm sense of pride.

Until he remembered that someone else would be living in it.

"Cole, I have to go. I'm getting another call."

"No problem. I'll call you when I can—for updates," he added belatedly.

"Talk to you then," she replied.

When they'd said their goodbyes, Cole eased back in his seat and watched through his windshield as customers entered and left through the Quick Stop's glass doors. This evening most of them were couples...walking two by two...some of them hand in hand. Maybe they'd be luckier than he and Margo had been.

Maybe they'd all stay as happy as they were tonight.

Wednesday was a blur. Margo buried herself in work, and tried not to think about Cole. In one week, he had become an integral part of her life again—and that wasn't healthy for her heart. Her heart didn't get any healthier when she spoke to Steve O'Dell about keeping a lid on confidential information. His anger was completely unexpected. So was his immediate request for personal time off. She'd tried to talk him out of it—tried to appeal to his sense of duty. They were in the middle of a murder investigation and they were already shorthanded. But in the end she knew if she didn't grant it, he'd suddenly come down with a case of "blue flu," and she'd be short-handed anyhow.

She'd mentioned it to Cole when he'd called that night, and though he was annoyed, he'd given Steve the benefit of the doubt. They'd all been working long hours, he'd said. Maybe O'Dell just needed to regroup.

On Thursday morning when Margo came into work, Sarah glanced up from her desk and sent her a nervous look. She picked up a similar look from blond, lanky Brett Johnson, who was speaking to someone on the phone. Her gaze rebounded to Sarah.

"Something going on?"

Grabbing the TV's remote, Sarah inched the volume up a notch, then rolled away from her desk and walked around it to Margo. She looked like a chubby daffodil this morning in a white blouse and bright yellow short-sleeved pantsuit that matched the headband holding back her red hair. "Steve's here," she murmured, fidgeting with the clunky zebra pendant she wore.

Margo glanced around. "Where?"

Sarah nodded toward the rear of the office, where the dark green door across from the interrogation room hung open. "He's in the locker room, picking up his stuff. He left an envelope on your desk."

Margo groaned in frustration, then strode to her desk. After opening the letter and glancing at the typewritten text, she tucked it back into the envelope.

Carrying a small duffel bag, Steve came back into the office, closing the door behind him. He was dressed in jeans and a rust-colored knit shirt.

Margo walked past the filing cabinets to meet him halfway. She showed him the envelope, kept her voice low. "What's this about, Steve?"

"Did you read it?"

"Yes."

"Then you know what it's about."

"Don't do this. You're a good cop, and we need you."

"Right. That's why you read me the riot act the other day."

Margo shook her head. "I didn't do that, and you know it. We had a conversation about confidential issues."

"Call it what you like," he returned. "I'm through feeling like excess baggage around here. The prodigal's returned. Manhattan can have his job back."

"This is about Cole?"

"Not totally."

"What else, then?"

"It doesn't matter," he said, cutting to the left and walking around her.

"It does matter," she said, following. "And I'm not accepting your resignation. Not until we talk things through."

Steve stopped at the spindled gate, nodded to Brett, who grimly nodded back, then turned to Margo. "Accept it or don't accept it. It's immaterial to me. I won't be back." He glanced at Sarah. "See you."

Sarah was still fidgeting with her zebra. "Take care of yourself."

When the door closed behind him, Sarah wandered through the gate, her blue eyes woeful behind her pink-tinted lenses. "What are you going to do now, honey?"

"You mean, what am I going to do now that we're permanently shorthanded in the middle of a murder investigation? Or what am I going to do with his letter of resignation?"

"Both."

Brett walked over to them. He wanted answers, too.

"The letter's going into a drawer until his personal time's up. Three days. Then I'll talk to him again and hope he changes his mind. This makes no sense. Where did he get the idea that Cole was even vaguely interested in coming back?"

Sarah exchanged an uneasy look with Brett. "I don't know. But you might have to see Steve a lot sooner than that if you want answers. He told us he's leaving town."

Brett spoke. "He was serious. That leaves you, me, Charlie and Fish to cover the department, 24/7. Council needs to do some fast hiring."

Margo nodded, still too shell-shocked for her mind to come up with an alternate solution.

Sarah seemed to have one.

Reaching inside the pocket of her short-sleeved jacket, she pulled out three fun-size bags of M&M's. "Here," she said passing them around like a doctor dispensing stress relievers. "There's a magnet on my fridge that says, 'There's no problem too big for God and chocolate.' Looks like it's time to put it to the test."

Margo's prayer didn't work.

Steve O'Dell did not walk back in and say that he'd reconsidered. Worse, a few minutes later when she tried to reach his cell phone, there was no answer and she had to leave a message. She left the same message at his home.

His reaction was totally bewildering. It was too over the top. Apparently he was dealing with several issues, but if he wouldn't share them, there was little she could do.

Tipping forward in her seat, she called Bernice Marshall at her antiques shop. "Madam Mayor," she said regretfully. "It's time to dig out the applications we have on file and start interviewing. We might've just lost another cop. I'm hoping he'll reconsider, but…"

"Okay," Bernice said, sighing. "Let's hear the details before I start calling council members."

Thankfully, Adam's prediction that the Gold Star Killer had moved on appeared to be correct. With the exception of Steve O'Dell's possible resignation, all was quiet for the next two days. Even the news media had moved on to the next story. The absence of a note or a "gift" from the killer wasn't unusual because he'd gone away before without any fanfare, and he'd stayed away for two years. Still, Margo couldn't help thinking that Charity was experiencing the calm before the storm.

She shared her thoughts with Cole when he phoned just before ten o'clock on Friday—the third night he'd been gone.

"I can't say I'm disappointed," he replied. "If he *is* gone, it would mean no more killings. But it would also mean he's slipped through our fingers again, even after throwing us a few bones. The thing that really rips me is, if he did get safely out of the area, he's got to be feeling pretty good about himself."

Margo murmured her agreement. She'd turned out her bedside lamp so she could talk to him in the dark again, shutting out everything in the world except the two of them. "We did hear something from the PSP today. There was nothing on either of the notes, but they found cat hair in the smashed cell phone."

"And the Hudsons have a cat."

"Yes, but so might our killer. They're making comparisons." She paused. "How's the job going?" And when are you coming back?

He answered as though he'd read her thoughts. "I'll be

back tomorrow." His tone cooled. "I'm through peeping through keyholes for a while. Mrs. XYZ's going to be a very wealthy woman when the courts get through with her cheating husband." He drew a breath. "So, I'll see you tomorrow around four?"

Margo's spirits sank. "No, I have to leave by three. My mom's coming in on a four thirty-five commuter flight tomorrow. After that—" She squeezed her eyes shut and finished with words that were all too similar to those she'd said to him in the past. "After that, I promised to spend an hour or so with her. We have a lot of catching up to do."

"Of course you do," he returned.

But there'd been no disapproval in his voice, and she continued, trying not to sound too hopeful—or God help her, too desperate. "We could have breakfast after church on Sunday—if you want."

"Or I can get out of here a little earlier and go to the airport with you."

Her initial happiness turned to uneasiness. Having Cole and her mother in the same vehicle for the better part of an hour might not be wise, considering their history. Still, she'd been missing him, and Cole and her mom had both hinted that the past was over. Maybe a face-to-face wouldn't be bad if she made sure they avoided topics that were best left forgotten.

"Okay," Margo replied, smiling again. "I'll see you tomorrow."

"Oh—one more thing. I've been meaning to ask how things went with Grayson Security."

He would have to ask. Margo started the countdown to detonation. "They're installing the security in a new bank. Monday's the earliest they can accommodate me."

The silence on the other end of the line seemed to stretch out forever. Margo waited for him to say that she should've called Grayson sooner, and that she was playing with fire, being so cavalier about her safety—which she wasn't. Then he stunned her by replying in a carefully modulated tone that probably took all of his patience. "I'll see you tomorrow around three. Take care."

Margo smiled. "Travel safely."

TWELVE

The small Dubois Regional Airport was a busy place at four o'clock when Margo parked her Cherokee in the lot and they got out. Crossing the lot to the buff-colored brick terminal, she and Cole joined commuters who'd apparently be taking the 4:50 p.m. flight to Cleveland. Cole ushered Margo through the double glass doors, then followed her inside the noisy café adjacent to the waiting area. The Flight Deck Restaurant was an open, high-ceilinged affair with an L-shaped lunch counter, standard tables and chairs and a few aeronautical touches. Historic photos crowded the wall on the right, and in one corner, airplane mobiles hung from the ceiling.

Spotting a booth near a glass wall with a view of the runway, Margo strode quickly toward it. When they were seated, they continued a conversation they'd begun on the way inside.

"You're surprised," Cole said.

"Maybe a little," she replied, hedging. Truthfully, she was more troubled by the news. Accepting Clete Banning's offer was one more thing that would keep Cole in Pittsburgh. "I guess I didn't expect that you'd be offered a partnership after such a short time with the firm."

His eyes twinkled. "Apparently, I'm good."

"Apparently," she repeated, summoning a smile. She dropped her gaze to the table to straighten the paper place mat and napkin-wrapped silverware in front of her. "Well, you wanted to work on feel-good projects. That should do it. You won't have to take assignments you dislike if you're the boss."

Cole frowned. "Actually, if I decide to accept, I'll lobby to cut the domestic stuff from our list of services. It would be a hard sell to Clete, though. The Seventh Commandment's violated so often that cheating's become one of the top moneymakers in our business. I'd still skip it. We're busy enough with missing persons and criminal investigations."

"Then maybe you should take Clete up on his offer," Margo returned, but only because it was the expected thing to say.

"That's what Sherry said, too—although she might not be with the agency much longer."

Margo held her response until a young blonde waitress wearing black slacks and a light mint sweater had taken their pie-and-coffee order. Then she asked curiously, "Sherry's leaving? I thought she liked working at Sharp."

"She does like working there. But the SWAN group just offered her a job. The pay would be about the same, but there'd be more satisfaction in the work she'd be doing. I don't see how she can turn it down."

The SWAN group? Margo thought happily. Sharp's secretary was the woman who'd been honored for her volunteer work with abused women? Sherry Arden had been Cole's dinner date last week?

Their waitress brought their coffee and coconut-cream pie, asked if they'd like anything else, then left when they smiled and assured her they had what they needed right now.

Margo returned to their discussion. "I'm happy for Sherry," she said honestly, touching her fork to the sky-high meringue. She remembered Sherry and her two kids. She also remembered that there was no chemistry between Sherry and Cole. They liked and respected each other, but they really were only friends—which she found totally confusing. Every time she looked at Cole, every time she met his dark eyes and beautiful smile, she felt such a rush of love and attraction that her heart raced and her knees went weak.

The PA system squawked to life, but the announcement was swallowed by a Sinatra tune and the noisy conversation inside the restaurant.

Margo sent Cole a blank look. "Did you get that?"

He shook his head. "The only word I could make out was 'delayed.'"

Putting down her fork, Margo went to the lunch counter to speak to a waitress who was adding vanilla ice cream to a slice of apple pie. There was glitter on her cheek.

"Excuse me," Margo said. "Did you hear that announcement?"

The waitress looked up. "Yes, the four thirty-five commuter's been delayed because of a minor equipment problem. But don't be alarmed. They'll have it in the air soon."

That wasn't comforting. Flying made her uneasy to begin with. "How minor?"

The waitress smiled. "You can ask at the desk for more information, but I'm sure it's nothing."

"Thanks." Margo returned to their booth. "Sorry," she said to Cole. "Looks like we might be here for a while. Mom's flight's been delayed. There was a minor equipment problem."

He pushed his empty plate aside. "Now you're worried."

"Not worried. Concerned."

Cole took her hand across the table. And some part of Margo hoped he'd used her uneasiness as an excuse to touch, to connect. Smiling, he laced his fingers through hers. "Want me to quote statistics to you again?"

"No, because you make them up as you go. No one believes a person has a better chance of striking oil in a flowerpot than falling out of an airplane."

"I never said how big the flowerpot had to be," he chuckled.

An hour passed, and Margo as well as a half-dozen others waiting for the 4:35 flight grew fidgety. She got up and walked to the doors facing the tarmac, looking for silver wings in the sky. She'd learned at the desk that her mother's plane had indeed left Cleveland. But she knew that wasn't the root of her stress. Suddenly she was extremely agitated about Cole and her mother's first meeting after more than a year.

She returned to her seat, tried to watch the wall-mounted television. Cole lowered the newspaper he'd bought from a dispenser. "They wouldn't have okayed the plane for takeoff if there were still problems. Relax."

"Doing my best," she replied.

A plane landed, a private jet carrying businessmen. Margo watched them cross the tarmac, talking among themselves, then enter and head directly for the exit and their waiting vehicles.

She checked her watch for the tenth time. "They're only a few minutes out now."

Cole folded his paper, placed it on the seat beside him.

"Okay, what's up? You're too wired tonight for it to be only the plane." Then his brow furrowed as something seemed to dawn on him. "You're afraid I'm going to say or do something that'll wreck your mother's homecoming, aren't you?"

Margo answered uncomfortably. "Not exactly. But over the past few days you've made some subtle references to our breakup."

"If I did, I wasn't aware of it."

She didn't see how that could be, but the mind was an annoyingly tricky thing. She drew a deep breath. "It's just that we have a long drive home. I don't want it to be an uncomfortable trip."

Cole got up and strolled to the long glass windows looking out on the landing strip, and Margo sighed, knowing it had been a mistake to bring it up.

When she walked over to stand beside him, he lowered his voice. "Do you really think I'd offer to come with you, then act like a jerk when your mom showed up?"

"No. But the last time you and my mother were together, you were—"

"Cold?"

"Yes."

"I meant to be. But my problems with her are in the past. I don't know how I can say this any plainer. I'm not going to dredge up old issues. They don't apply anymore. That's not why I came with you tonight."

"Why did you come?" *Please say it's because you wanted to be with me.*

He paused for a few seconds, then glanced away, almost as though he didn't want to answer the question. "Because I didn't want you driving here alone. He could still be out there, and you could still be a target. Our relationship's different now, but I still want you to see your grandkids grow up."

A lump rose in her throat, but she managed a flippant response. "Well, since I have zero matrimonial prospects, it's going to be pretty tough to have kids, let alone grandkids."

"You know what I mean," he said seriously. "I want you to be around for a very long time. As for your having no prospects, I suspect that's a temporary condition." His gaze drifted over her long hair, scoop-neck raspberry sweater and white slacks, then he mustered a faint smile. "You're beautiful and you're smart. There's someone out there for you."

Was there really? she thought, her eyes on the runway in the distance. Once upon a time, her mother told her to never settle for anything less than a man she loved with all her heart. It was still sound advice today. If she couldn't have Cole, she didn't want anyone.

"They're on their way in," the guard at the desk called to them. "An hour and forty minutes late, but they made it." He chuckled. "Have a good evening, everybody."

Have a good evening? The plane touched down and taxied toward them, and she and Cole backed away from the doors. The man had no idea how difficult that would be.

From a distance, Cole watched Margo pull out of her mother's driveway and continue to the intersection— where vigilant Fish waited to follow her home. Pulling on his lights, Cole moved from the side of the road, then proceeded toward Charlotte McBride's traditional white two-story with the black shutters. Margo had dropped him off at the Blackberry just after 7:00 p.m., but the thoughts churning through his mind had made it impossible to work. It bugged him that he'd had no opportunity to say the things he wanted to say to Charlotte with Margo present. Now he could.

Parking in the street, he shut off the engine and got out. In the carefully manicured yard, a tall black lamppost shone brightly, its base surrounded by clusters of orange-and-yellow marigolds. Close to the house, solar lights ringed the roses, hollies and golden bayberries.

Cole climbed the front stoop and rang the bell. To say she was flustered to see him was an understatement.

"Cole?" she said. "You...you missed Margo. She just left."

"I'm not here to see Margo," he replied. "I'm here to see you."

She seemed unable to say anything for a moment, then she opened the door and he stepped inside. "I was just having a cup of tea before bed," she said, her searching gaze clearly wondering what he wanted. "Can I pour you a cup, too?"

"No, thanks. What I have to say won't take long."

"All right," she replied, nodding toward the kitchen where her teakettle had begun to shriek. "Just let me turn off the kettle, and we'll talk."

Cole wiped his boots on the rug in front of the door— unnecessarily—then followed her through her berry-and-gray living room to the kitchen. Charlotte was a fifty-seven-year-old, slightly heavier version of her pretty daughter, with chin-length auburn hair and—almost— the same green eyes. But Charlotte's eyes lacked the confidence and conviction he usually saw in Margo's.

She turned off the gas burner, sighed and faced him. Her turquoise-and-white tracksuit was designed to be comfortable, but she looked anything but. "What did you want to talk about?"

Cole softened his voice. "Margo didn't want me to say anything that might spoil your homecoming tonight, so I didn't. We all did a good job of ignoring our mutual history. But not talking about it took away my chance to say that I'm sorry for the way I treated you back then."

Her lips parted, but she remained silent.

"Anyway," he went on. "I sensed that you were waiting for the other shoe to drop when there were a few quiet moments on the way home. I just want to assure you that both of my shoes—" He smiled and corrected himself. "—both of my boots, are staying on my feet. Margo and I are friends again. I hope we can be friends, too."

She couldn't have hidden her relief if she'd tried. "Thank you for that," she murmured, then her voice strengthened. "Margo said the same thing to me. She said just let things go, and they'll take care of themselves. But you know what? Sometimes you can't." She glanced at her clasped hands—twisted her wide, gold wedding band on her finger before she looked up again. "We all did what we felt we had to do back then, Cole. But I was the selfish one, and I can't tell you how deeply I regret that. I hurt you, and I hurt my own daughter—the person I love most in this world. I'll never forgive myself for what I cost the two of you."

Cole shook his head. "Margo made her own decisions."

"No, she didn't. I left her no choice." Swallowing, she took a few steps toward him. "I've talked to her about this—asked if there was a chance the two of you might be able to..." She let the sentence trail. "But she tells me you both have different lives now, and that you're happy the way things are."

Was she happy? Or had she only said that to soothe her mother's guilt? As for him, he wasn't happy, but he was doing okay, and that might be all he could expect. It was better than some people got.

He checked his wristwatch. It was only a few minutes after nine, but Charlotte looked tired. "It's late," he said with a smile, then extended his hand to her. "I'll get out of here now and let you get some sleep."

She squeezed his hand between both of hers. "Come to dinner tomorrow night."

He was touched, but that wasn't a good idea. "I can't, Charlotte, but thanks. I'm starting a new case, and I need to get the preliminaries taken care of before I start the legwork."

"Then let's make it another night this week if the two of you can get away. I brought back souvenirs for both of you when Margo said you were working together again on this horrible case." She paused. "Thank you for that, by the way. I worry about her."

So did he.

"How about Tuesday or Wednesday?" she pressed. "You always liked my chicken Parmesan."

It was impossible not to smile again. "I'll try, but I can't promise. Have a good night."

"You, too."

He'd just started his truck and was preparing to leave when his cell phone thumped out the *Peter Gunn* theme. Cole took the phone from the case on his belt and checked the screen: Margo's home phone number.

"Margo?"

"Hi," she said. "I hope I didn't wake you."

This early? Then again, who slept anymore? "No, I still have some work to do before I hit the sack. What's up?"

"When we spoke on Friday night, I mentioned having breakfast after church tomorrow, then we started talking about picking up my mom and never got back to it. I thought I'd better check with you before I made other plans. Are you interested or do you want to pass?"

Cole stared out at the dark sky beyond the streetlights, looking for some intestinal fortitude, then discovered he was fresh out. He was an idiot. He was a raving lunatic who should have his head examined, because no one in the world would ever be as stupid as he was about to be. But if the Gold Star Killer was in the wind, he wouldn't be seeing much of her anymore. He'd be heading back to Pittsburgh for good—and soon-to-be Chief McBride would be getting on with her happy life.

"Sounds doable," he said. "I'll grab something from the bakery early, before everything's all picked over."

"Good idea," she said. "I'll see you in the morning."

"Yep, see you then."

Scowling, Cole tucked his phone back in its case, dropped the truck into gear and hit the gas pedal. He wasn't just stupid. He was like that proverbial moth. He just couldn't wait to have his wings singed again.

Shutting off the spray, Margo got out of the shower, wrapped herself in her white terry robe and towel dried her hair. Once again, Charity had had a quiet night, according to Brett whom she'd phoned a while ago. That was one more thing to be thankful for this sunny Sunday morning. She plugged in her hair dryer, finger fluffed her hair in the mirror, then turned on the heat. Her hair was still damp when she thought she heard banging at the door and someone shouting her name. Frowning, she shut off the dryer.

"Margo!" More staccato banging. "Margo, open up!"

Alarmed now, she rushed from the bathroom, followed

the incessant shouting to her kitchen entry and threw open the door. He stepped inside. "Cole, what's wrong?"

She'd never seen fear like that in his eyes. "Thank God, you're okay." He tossed a bakery bag on the counter. "I have the station on speed dial, so I've already talked to Brett. He's alerting the PSP."

Margo's pulse thudded in her ears. Please, God—no more dead girls. "What happened?"

Tugging her by the hand, he led her outside, past the vehicles in her driveway, then stopped in front of her porch. The air left her lungs.

A line of five tiny gold stars winked in the sunlight hitting her front door.

She'd been marked.

A half hour later, Margo cringed to see her street flooded with cops, cruisers, flashing lights and more neighbors with craning necks than she'd ever seen, many of them on cell phones. Even Cole had a cell phone in hand, and his conversation looked deadly serious. Dear God. She'd never keep this quiet. All they needed now was a massive explosion and they'd have a Bruce Willis film. Jenna, who had a bird's-eye view of it all, had called earlier. Even Ollie Murdock had shown up and was frantically snapping pictures. He'd told her a few minutes ago that all bets were off. All the details, including a copy he'd made of that poetic "raise the bar" note, would run in the morning paper.

There was no defusing the situation now.

She'd decided to issue a statement this evening at six, and had Sarah contact the area media. Hopefully, it would be picked up by a few network affiliates because she wanted their star-studded freak to see it. They were through playing games. They needed to draw him out, make him do something foolish so they could finish this once and for all.

She trusted the department with her safety; they were uneasy with her decision, but in complete agreement that a press conference that attacked the man's pride and instability was the way to go. All except Cole, who'd insisted that Margo was setting herself up as bait. But their cowardly killer had a specific signature and she had to trust that, too. He acted at night in secluded places, and he preferred to strangle, not shoot. Logic dictated that if he couldn't get close, she'd be safe.

"Okay," Cole said grimly when the cruisers had cleared out and she'd finished alerting her mother. "What do you plan to say in your statement?"

Margo walked around her kitchen, arms folded, trying to arrange her thoughts. She'd had a sundress and white sandals laid out for church, but when she knew she wouldn't make the service, she'd pulled on navy chinos and a red-and-white striped knit top. "I'm not sure. I'm still trying to decide what kinds of things will really push his buttons."

"I'll get my laptop from Jenna's place, then I'll be back. When you get hungry we can call for takeout."

Margo studied his grave expression. "You're not leaving?"

"Fish and Brett said they've been practically joined at the hip with you lately, yet someone still managed to stick those stars to your door. I'll stay as long as I'm able, or until you throw me out." He nodded toward the front of her house. "I put a sign out there a few minutes ago, and I've phoned Sherry. She's driving up with the electronics equipment I'll need. You might as well cancel Grayson Security."

Signs? Electronics? Margo strode through the house,

then outside to stand on the sidewalk facing her porch. The ten-by-fifteen-inch burgundy-and-white sign wired to the white lattice was tasteful and succinct in its message: Premises Protected by Sharp, Inc.

She looked quizzically at Cole, who'd followed her as far as the porch. Then she ascended the steps to speak to him. "You just happened to have one of these lying around?"

His chiseled features and dark eyes were as stern as she'd ever seen them. "I put it in the truck after you told me Grayson wasn't coming until Monday. If I'd remembered to wire it to your porch last night—"

"—we wouldn't have more evidence to examine." Margo's gaze strayed to her white screen door. She'd wiped away the powder after the prints had been photographed and collected, but a few dark smudges still remained. There were more advanced ways of collecting prints. But for the money, old-fashioned black powder was still one of the most effective methods. She smiled her appreciation at Cole. "The sign's great. Thank you."

"You're welcome. Tomorrow I'll install cameras and wireless alarms, front and back. I should've done it long before this." He drew a deep breath. "I suppose you know that Fish and Charlie want to take turns bunking on your couch."

"I know," Margo replied. "They're sweet. Jenna and Rachel offered, too, and my mom practically ordered me to stay with her. But I won't put them at risk."

She chewed her lip for a moment. "But would they really be at risk? I know you probably don't want to hear this, Cole, but part of me still wonders if this is just look-at-me grandstanding. He has to be ticked off that we kept his last note away from the media. Maybe he's filling a scrapbook and wants more clippings. We both know I'm the wrong age for this guy, and I'm far from blonde."

"Anything's possible," Cole replied, and from the look on his face, she knew he'd considered that, too. "I'm still installing the alarms."

Margo had finished at the computer forty minutes later when the phone in her home office rang. Charity P.D. appeared in the caller ID window. Margo picked up, listened to Fish's somber message, then spoke quietly. "Okay, we'll see you out there." Sick at heart, she hung up, then rose from her chair and went into the kitchen. Cole was at the table, working on an expense sheet.

"I told you about the kids who ripped up the field near Elmer's house on their four-wheelers, didn't I?"

Cole stood. "Is Elmer okay?"

Margo nodded. "But the kids were out riding again this morning. One of them had a cell phone and called the station. Cole, someone smashed the front windows in your house."

His face turned to stone.

"I'm so sorry," she said, taking her keys from the kitchen counter. "Doing something like this is so juvenile. When I get my hands on the kids who—"

"What if it wasn't kids?" he interjected. "What if someone has an ax to grind with me? Or wants to get to you through me?"

Margo searched his eyes.

"I need to say something, and I don't want you to get upset. I'm not accusing anyone of anything. I'm just trying to keep an open mind."

"What are you talking about?"

Cole drew a breath, then spoke with some reluctance. "Who do we know who's been acting irrationally lately?

Someone who's not a big fan of mine. Is there a very small…let me repeat that…a very small chance that someone just raised the bar?"

Margo shook her head insistently. "No. He wouldn't."

"I don't want to think that, but he was the person who discovered the first note."

"No," she said again. "He's too old, and he's not from this part of Pennsylvania."

"The profile's just a guide. And there's still a chance that the Hudson case was a copycat."

Margo shook her head again. Vandalism maybe, but not murder. She knew Steve better than Cole did, and it would take an act of God to make her believe he was guilty of anything other than bad judgment. "I don't believe he smashed your windows, and I *won't* believe he hurt the Hudson girl. But I'll talk to him." And when she was through, she'd kiss goodbye any chance of him returning to the department.

If the vandalism was related to the murder case, there was no evidence to support it. No gold stars, no silky scarves. Just a lot of smashed glass and more than a dozen rocks Cole himself had supplied. The rock pile on the left side of the house was almost depleted.

Now Cole was at a building-supply house buying plywood to board up the place, and Margo was back at the station. She'd felt sick watching him assess the damages. He'd put months of backbreaking work and love into creating the home they would've lived in.

Sadly, there was little chance that restitution would be made. Mookie and his posse had gunned their four-wheelers up and down the driveway, obliterating any other tracks, and the rocks surrounding the house left nothing in the way of traceable footprints. Their best hope of finding the person who'd done this was word of mouth. Some perps just had to brag. And some people who heard the story just had to turn them in.

At six o'clock the parking lot outside the police station was a media circus of cameras, reporters with microphones and news vans. Behind the media, onlookers pressed close.

Margo descended the steps with her notes, thanked them all for coming and began to speak. Some of what she planned to say was inflammatory and dead wrong. But her main reason for calling this press conference was to reel in the killer. She'd set the record straight later.

"I doubt I have to preface my remarks by telling you what's been going on here recently, so I'll just bring you up to date. We've had some contact from the Gold Star Killer. We received two notes that failed to yield fingerprints or fibers, but luckily for us—and unluckily for him—sometime last night he placed five gold stars on my front door."

Murmurs swept through the crowd, though Margo suspected the information wasn't news to anyone.

"Several prints were recovered from the door, and they—as well as the stars—are currently being examined at the state police lab. We feel confident that we'll have good news for the community soon. That said, time is of the utmost importance so I'd like to describe this loser in the hope that one of your readers, listeners or viewers will recognize him and notify us. Also, I'm sorry, but I won't be taking questions afterward."

She drew a breath, scanned the crowd and the cameras—and wondered if he was among those intently watching her. She hoped so. She dearly hoped so.

"We believe he's a white male between the ages of eighteen and thirty-two, with at least a high-school education. He probably lost a parent early in life, and spends much of his time alone. He has few male friends. Those he has are as unstable as he is."

She looked over the crowd again. "His few involvements with women have failed. Something about him—his appearance, possibly his intellect—makes it difficult for him to compete with normal men. We believe that most women find him unattractive."

God, forgive me for stretching the truth, but this is the only way. You can punish me later for my lies.

She consulted her notes, then lowered the sheet and finished, letting her gaze touch every reporter, every cameraman, every spectator. "We're dealing with a bottom-feeder, a dim-witted coward who's inadequate in almost everything he tries. So look around, people, and call us if you think you know someone who meets this description. Your name will be held in strictest confidence."

From his position to the left of the crowd, Brett looked uneasy, as did Fish and Charlie, who were stationed on the other side. Then Margo spotted a tall man in a baseball cap, dark glasses and an olive-drab camouflage shirt…and felt a chill when it appeared he was staring back.

"That's it," she said, wrapping things up. "Thanks for your time."

Everyone started speaking at once, thrusting microphones, pressing closer. But Margo shook her head. "Sorry, but I told you at the beginning that I wouldn't be taking questions. Thanks again."

Turning away, she lowered her voice and glanced at Cole, who was waiting to the right of the door. "See the tall guy in the sunglasses and camouflage near the street?"

"Already spotted him," he said, opening the door for her. "I'm on it."

"Thanks. Now let's hope one of the million calls we're expecting pays off."

THIRTEEN

The guy in the camouflage shirt and shades wasn't their killer. He was a piece of work, but in the end, he was the type who'd be too arrogant to hide in the dark until a potential victim came along. Wade Renshaw, whom they'd actually considered as they'd gone through their "troublemaker files" the second time, would do it in broad daylight. But Renshaw's talent was stealing cars. He wouldn't kill. Still, they were keeping an eye on him, waiting to see who he hung out with.

"I thought you'd have a cast on your ear when I picked you up," Cole said, lifting a section of plywood to the last of his empty window frames. "How many phone calls did you get?"

Margo steadied her side of the plywood. "Only twelve. The PSP got a few, too."

Pinning the wood with his left shoulder, he grabbed a hammer and nails from a makeshift table. "Sure that's not too heavy?"

"Actually, it feels lighter than the last one. I must be getting tougher."

He smiled. "Yeah, you're tough, all right. Just hold on for another minute." He drove in a half-dozen nails, the staccato banging temporarily drowning out the sound of the generator.

"We'll be swamped with calls in the morning, though," she said when he'd finished. "Nancy Talbot called just before you picked me up. She said my statement would run at eleven o'clock, then again during their daybreak segment at six and seven. She asked if there was anything further that I'd like to add. When I said no, she asked me to fax her a copy of the 'raise the bar' note to show her viewers, but I couldn't do that to Ollie."

"She's dedicated," he noted sarcastically, then came to Margo's side of the window casing. Gripping the hammer, he banged the rest of the nails home, then backed up a few paces and stared. It wasn't a defeated look that he wore. It was a look of grim acceptance. Margo couldn't imagine him giving up on anything. Except the two of them.

"When will the new windows be in?"

"Two weeks."

Nodding, sensing the bleakness he wouldn't show her, Margo closed the distance between them and took his free hand. "It's fixable."

Cole dropped the hammer and gathered her close, and for a few moments, they stood there, listening to the night wind blow.

"I know," he said finally, setting her back from him. "I wish everything was."

Was this the opening they'd been waiting for? Margo's hopeful heart stepped up its pace, but she remained silent, afraid to say something that would change the direction of his thoughts.

"I went to see your mother last night after you left her," he said quietly. "I apologized for the things I said before. We had a good talk. She invited me to dinner."

It took all the energy she had to keep her hopefulness under control. If he'd smoothed things over with her mother, maybe... "Did you accept?"

"Tentatively. But now it looks like I'll be on the road for the next couple of days. There was a price on the electronics package Sherry dropped off. Clete wants me in the office at ten tomorrow morning."

Margo's burgeoning spirits sank. "But you just got back."

He shrugged. "He's the boss until I accept the partnership. Then I'll have some control. He's bringing another P.I. aboard and wants me to sit in on two interviews. Then on Friday there's a party for Sherry. She's taking the job with SWAN."

She was getting so weary of her pathetic, flip-flopping emotions. Maybe it was time to face facts—for both of them. She'd been wrong when she'd told Cole that commuting between Charity and Pittsburgh was an option. It wouldn't have worked. Already, she could see lines of fatigue around his dark eyes. A man couldn't keep burning the candle at both ends and not expect to burn out. "Maybe you should stay there this time," she said quietly.

He didn't speak for a moment. "You want me to go?"

"I don't want you constantly driving the roads, sleep deprived and distracted. You're spreading yourself too thin. This case isn't worth sacrificing your health...or worse."

"I need this case, Margo. I can't let it go."

"I know." It had been easier for him to let go of her.

"And I don't want to go back. Especially now that you've stirred things up. I just don't have a choice. I'll install the alarms before I leave in the morning."

"Cole—"

He touched his index finger to her lips. "I can handle it. It won't take long. Call if anything comes up. I should be back before three."

Taking her hand, he led her across the dusty subfloor to where an old blanket lay and a lamp burned, courtesy of the noisy generator on the porch.

"Have a seat. We have time for cocoa before we head back."

She nearly said, "Sounds good," just for something to say. But that would've been a lie. Once again, they'd missed an opportunity to talk things through—to get everything out in the open and finally say all the things that had gone unsaid for nearly a year. And she was too big a coward to steer the conversation back to that subject.

Margo curled herself onto the fringed red, green and tan plaid picnic blanket they used to take to the river, and Cole dropped down beside her. Easing his back to the wall, he grabbed the thermos next to him, removed the cap and took out the smaller cup nested inside. He filled the cups.

Cole handed her the larger one and raised his to hers, the sweet smell of steaming hot chocolate wafting upward and holding her heart hostage yet again. She couldn't stop the memories.

"Feels like déjà vu, doesn't it?" he said.

"More than a little bit," she replied. "Go ahead. You make the toast."

"Okay," he said quietly. "To forgiveness. I made some mistakes, Margo. I shouldn't have pressured you. I should've done a lot of things differently." His tender gaze touched hers. "I want to wipe the slate clean."

It was the perfect toast, healing words that, a few

minutes ago, would've sent her heart soaring. But she was finally wise enough not to read too much into them. "We both made mistakes. I should've found a way to say yes to you more often."

"But it's all behind us now."

"Yes," she said. "It's all behind us."

The generator growled on, covering any sound their plastic cups made as they touched them together and said the words.

"To forgiveness."

True to his word, Cole was at her home before six the next morning to install wireless alarms and tiny cameras at every entry. Then he was gone again. Margo left shortly afterward to get some work done before the phones started ringing.

Now, as she hung up and added another name and address to the already incredible list of potential suspects on the yellow legal pad in front of her, she considered Murphy's Law: anything that could go wrong would— and it had.

Forty minutes ago, Charlie's wife had called with the happy-nervous news that their daughter was in labor and on her way to the hospital. Despite his lukewarm protestations, Margo told Charlie to get over to the hospital. He was Ginny's Lamaze coach. So with Steve gone, Fish getting some sleep after working hoot-owl and Brett on the outskirts of Charity waiting to escort a wide load through town, only she and Sarah were available to man the phones.

Margo perused her list of "suspects" again and shook her head. People were reporting their mail delivery men *and women,* their relatives and their "too spooky for words" next-door neighbors. Some of the calls weren't even from the area, but people seemed willing to pay the long-distance charges for an opportunity to vent.

She got up and threw away the half-eaten, two-hour-old BLT she'd ordered for lunch. She was grabbing a Pepsi from the fridge when her phone rang again. She strode back to her desk wondering who the new "suspect" would be.

"Charity Police Department," she said, snatching up the receiver.

The voice on the phone was old and grumpy, but in a friendly way. "I'd like to talk to your acting chief, missy."

Margo smiled at the term, then said, "Speaking. What can I do for you?"

"You can put my mind at ease and tell me that our two murders aren't related. I'm Chief of Police Ham Jarvis. We're in a little Podunk town about the size of yours, halfway between Philly and Wilkes-Barre. I was watchin' the news last night when your statement ran." He exhaled shortly. "We've got some serious similarities."

Margo tipped forward in her chair, blotting out the low hum of CNN and the other conversation in the room. "Was your victim a small blonde woman in her late teens or early twenties?"

"She was."

"When did your murder take place, Chief?"

"November of last year. It was a strangulation case. There were no stars on the body, but the perp wrapped a scarf around the vic's neck when he was done with her."

Margo's pulse stepped up its pace. "A silk scarf?"

"No, this one was one of those striped, knitted mufflers the kids around here wear in the cold weather."

"Did he use his hands?"

"He did. We have photos of the bruises. You might want to compare them to yours. I can send them to you straightaway."

"Thank you. I'd appreciate that."

"You'll let me know what you find?"

"Immediately." Margo rattled off the department's fax number, then, trapping the receiver between her ear and shoulder, she flipped to a new page on her legal pad and picked up her pen. "Let me jot down your address and phone number—though I guess I can get that from caller ID." Even if there were no stars present, there was a chance they'd found the third victim. "Okay, you said that you're Chief Ham Jarvis."

"That's right. Ham for Hamlet." He chuckled. "My ma, God rest her soul, loved Shakespeare."

Margo smiled. "And where exactly are you located?"

"Port Crenshaw, PA."

Margo frowned as she wrote it, wondering why that town sounded familiar, then continued. "Okay, Chief, I'll get back to you as soon as I can. Give me a little while, though. I'll want the state police to do the measurements and comparisons."

"Good enough. Talk to you later."

"Oh—one more thing. We checked ViCAP and every other database we could think of but we didn't—"

"—run across my case. I know," he said, the warmth leaving his tone. "We had a mix-up. It was never entered."

There wasn't much she could say to that. "I'll watch for the photos. Thanks again."

Margo hung up, the name of the town continuing to niggle at her. She plumbed her memory for a minute more, then decided there was an easier way to figure it out. Swiveling in her chair, she typed the town's name into her PC while she waited for the fax to come in. The screen filled with a pretty header followed by various statistics: Port Crenshaw's area, population, nearness to events, churches and…schools.

Margo struggled to take her next breath.

Dear God, no. Please, let this be a terrible coincidence.

Blood pounding in her temples, she strode to the storage room, pulled out the box she'd filled only yesterday and dropped to her knees. She dug through it, tossing books and papers to the floor. Toiletries and a leather shaving kit joined the pile, followed by a man's black tie with a tie tack still attached, tiny silver handcuffs dangling from the post.

Please, God, please.

She pulled out the day planner. Flipped through the pages—found nothing. Then a plain black-and-white embossed business card fell out and fluttered to the floor. It landed perfectly. She didn't have to turn it over to read the name, number and address.

Dr. Miles Bellamy
Psychiatric Medicine

John Wilcox's chuckling voice came back to her. *"It's just a little town, only a couple miles from the college. There's a diner there that has the best sticky walnut rolls this side of your grandma's kitchen."*

Margo stayed there for a moment, her senses reeling, her mind refusing to believe what it must. Then she placed the items back in the box and took the business card to her desk. The TV still droned on—someone reporting that the Dow was up sixteen points. Sarah's chirpy phone voice sounded the same. Nothing had changed, and suddenly everything had changed.

Margo picked up the phone and dialed. In a moment, a cordial feminine voice came on the line. "Good afternoon. Doctor Bellamy's office."

With a heavy heart, Margo identified herself then said, "It's urgent that I speak to the doctor about one of his patients. If he needs verification please tell him to check the listings for the Charity Police Department in Charity, Pennsylvania, and call me back."

"May I tell him what this is in reference to?"

"A homicide investigation."

Dr. Bellamy did call her back. Their conversation only took a minute. She was hanging up when Sarah pushed open the spindled gate and walked slowly to Margo's desk, a troubled look on her usually sunny face.

"First of all, Cole just called. He's only fifteen minutes out."

Thank You, God.

"And this just came in." She extended two sheets of fax paper. "It's from the chief of police in Port Crenshaw."

Margo accepted the sheets. "Thanks, Sarah."

"Port Crenshaw," she said nervously. "Isn't that where…"

"Yes, it is."

Her eyes filled with tears. "Oh, Margo."

"I know. Call Brett and get him in here. And get Fish out of bed."

"What about Charlie?"

"Charlie's busy with his daughter."

Margo picked up the phone again. Cole answered. "Yeah, Sarah?"

"It's not Sarah, it's me," Margo said, unable to keep

the sorrow from her voice as she filled him in; she could hear the disappointment in his when she'd finished.

"And since John was already gone when the last murder occurred, unless you're dealing with a coincidence of unbelievable magnitude…"

"Yes. It's Adam. It will be a lot easier if he comes to us. If not, then I guess we'll do it the hard way."

"Wait for me."

"I will if I can."

Hanging up, she tapped in Adam's number. When he answered, he sounded out of breath.

Margo forced a cheerfulness she didn't feel. "Adam, hi. It's Margo. I'm so glad I caught you at home. Is there any chance you can stop by the station this afternoon to pick up your dad's stuff? I finally got around to boxing it up yesterday."

"Sorry, but I'm kind of busy. Can it wait?"

No, she was afraid it couldn't. "Are you sure you can't step out for a few minutes? I'd really like to talk to you."

"About what?"

Her mind spun, then came up with a logical reply. "I've been thinking about our talk on Tuesday night. I'm concerned."

"Why?"

"Because I care about you."

For a long moment, there was nothing but empty air on the line. Then he spoke again, his tone cool. "Just give my dad's stuff away. I have more than enough memories to deal with."

Intuition flared. He'd seen her news conference.

"Adam—"

"Goodbye, Margo," he said. "I'm going back to school."

Margo hung up, her stomach roiling, her mind on fire. Was he? Was he going back to school, or was he running? And how soon was he leaving? He'd said he was busy. Was he packing? Pushing to her feet, she called to Sarah. "Did you get hold of Brett and Fish?"

"Brett's on his way. I can't reach Fish. There's no answer at his place, and his cell phone's not turned on."

"Call Brett again," she said, breezing through the gate and heading for the door. "Tell him to meet me at the Wilcox place."

"Be careful," Sarah fretted.

"I will," she called back, then pushed through the door and hurried to her black-and-white. She pulled out her cell phone. "Cole, I just spoke to Adam. I'm on my way to his place. So is Brett. I think he's going to run."

"I'll see you there," he said tersely. "Don't go in without backup. I'm still ten minutes away."

The Wilcoxes' beige-and-white ranch house was the lone residence at the end of the sparsely populated country road, and appeared to spring from the grass and fields that surrounded it. Thick woods rose at the back of the sprawling acreage. To the left, barbed-wire fencing separated properties, and behind and to the right of the house, a utility shed sat beside a detached garage with the same beige vinyl siding.

John's late-model navy SUV was parked in the gravel driveway close to the house.

Margo sat tensely in the prowl car forty yards from the Wilcox's driveway, hidden behind a wall of pines lining the road. She checked her wristwatch, then raised her binoculars again, focusing on a break between the heavy boughs.

Adrenaline jolted her as Adam left the house carrying

a bulging trash bag and a soft suitcase, then moved quickly down the porch steps to the car. Margo's heartbeat accelerated.

Where were Brett and Cole? They should've been here by now.

The front door was ajar, so he was obviously going back inside, but how many more trips would he make before he grabbed his keys and was gone?

He retraced his steps to the house.

Margo lowered the field glasses, blood pounding in her temples. She couldn't wait much longer. She had to act soon, and God help her, she didn't want to. She'd known Adam since he was a thin, quiet, bespectacled boy of thirteen—had liked him, always took an interest in what he was doing, always asked about his grades and his hobbies—though there never seemed to be any. He'd needed that kind of support with his mother gone and John working so much. Still, she'd never taken the time to make his life happier.

But would it have done any good? Was it nature or nurture? Did serial killers spring from the womb, or were they shaped by their surroundings? Could she or John or anyone else have done anything differently to change this tragic series of events?

She couldn't wait.

Dropping the car into gear, she sped up the road, turned down the driveway and brought the cruiser up tightly against the SUV's back bumper.

Whispering a prayer that force wouldn't be necessary, she got out. She couldn't let him get into the car. His driveway exit was blocked, but there was nothing but grass and fields in front of the SUV, and it would be no problem for him to drive around the house to access the road.

Fear collected in her throat.

She unsnapped the holster on her hip.

He strangles. He doesn't shoot.

He's had opportunities to hurt me. He didn't.

Adam opened the door and smiled. "Margo," he called, carrying a box of perishable food out of the house. The late-day sun shone on his surfer hair as he came down the porch steps. "What's up?"

What's up? "You tell me," she called back.

Sighing, he came toward her, the box in his arms. "This is about your phone call, isn't it? I'm sorry," he said forlornly. "I was just—"

Cole's truck roared into view and Adam's tone went cold and flat. "I really am sorry."

Everything happened in a flash. He dropped the box and his fist flew at her face.

Margo yanked out her Glock. *God, help me!* Fired.

Stars exploded in her head as Adam screamed and the hard ground rushed up to meet her.

Electric. His fear was electric. *Please, God! Let her be okay!*

Cole gunned the truck down the driveway, his pulse on fire—saw to his relief that Margo was scrambling to her feet. He shifted his focus. Adam was running, racing toward the high, overgrown field and the dense woods behind it. Bright red blood bloomed on the thigh of his long khaki shorts.

Another cruiser came down the uneven drive behind him. *Brett.*

Cole swerved to the right, bounced into the grass beside the cruiser—cut sharply in front of Adam's SUV and blocked it in.

Cole leaped out and hit the ground running, crashing through the long grass and thick goldenrods, handcuffs clanking against his hip. Adam was forty yards ahead of him, panting, whining in pain. Cole accelerated, closing the distance between them, briars catching his jeans and cutting his hands and arms. Adam knew these woods better than they did. If he got to the trees—

"Adam, stop! I don't want to shoot!"

He kept running.

Cole yanked his gun from the back of his jeans—fired a warning shot over Adam's head.

The kid stopped.

Gasping, turning around a dozen yards from the tree line, Adam squeezed his eyes shut, then put his hands in the air.

Sick to his soul, Cole hurried forward, checked the kid's wound and saw that it was only a crease—and thank God for that—then he pulled Adam's hands behind his back and cuffed him. He had no words for the kid. Margo and Brett were hurrying through the grass and tall goldenrods. It was up to them to advise Adam of his Miranda rights and ask the big question: Why?

Adam looked away, his face lined in pain, something desperate in his voice. "Don't let her near me. I'll go with Brett. I can't talk to her."

"Why not?"

He looked away.

But somehow Cole knew. Adam still cared enough about Margo to spare her the disappointment of arresting him…and at the same time, spare himself the humiliation of admitting what he'd done. Could Margo's instincts have been right? Was there a possibility that she'd never been in mortal danger? Just before Margo and Brett reached them, Adam turned to Cole and quietly filled in the answer.

"I just wanted to scare her off. She was nice to me."

That night, Margo rested her head against the back of her sofa while Cole held a cold pack wrapped in a washcloth to the reddish-blue bruise on her jaw. She was exhausted and utterly heartsick over Adam's confession, and the soothing country song coming from the radio in the kitchen wasn't helping. When Adam waived his right to an attorney, they realized that they'd been correct when they'd considered that their killer wanted to get caught. Some part of Adam had wanted this to be over. His insistence that his killings were justifiable and his admission that he'd smashed Cole's windows said something else. If the courts decided to be merciful, Adam would be hospitalized for a very long time.

"You're still thinking about Adam," Cole said quietly, taking the cold pack from her jaw. A few strands of her hair had somehow gotten under the compress, and he brushed them back.

"I can't help it. I keep remembering that the first two victims were compassionate girls. They were church-goers—always helped out with food drives and other benefits. I know what Adam said, but I can't believe they ridiculed him."

"They probably didn't. After he asked them out and they turned him down, he probably relived their refusals, twisting things around in his mind until he'd created a scenario that just wasn't true." Cole sighed. "Then it was goodbye teenage crush, hello vengeance."

Margo straightened to meet his eyes, her heart full of love for him despite her low mood. "I'm glad you were there today."

"Me, too. It helped me close a door. I'm just sorry it was Adam."

Margo nodded. After John Wilcox found silk scarves in his son's room and confronted him, Adam promised his dad that the killings were over and agreed to see Dr. Bellamy. But the urge was too powerful to resist. His rage became uncontainable when his blonde college classmate turned him down, too. He'd had no stars to mark the event that time.

"He's not well, Margo," Cole said softly.

"I know," she returned. "He said Leanne was the biggest tease in their senior class, yet she'd never gone to school here."

"And his college girlfriend never existed."

Margo got up—walked to the window and looked out on a town that could finally put this horror behind them. "It still makes me angry that John knew and didn't bring him in."

Cole joined her at the window. "He loved his son. He couldn't bear the thought of him living out his life in a prison cell."

"You can't believe John's protection was justified."

"I don't. I'm just saying that John loved his son."

He truly had, but it had cost two more young women their lives. A chill moved through her as she heard Adam's defensive tone again.

"I've been teased my whole life. Kids made fun of my zits, my glasses—even my weight. Those girls needed to know that there are consequences. I didn't do anything wrong."

Cole opened his arms and drew Margo close. "Stop thinking about it. It won't change anything. Now that Adam's finally being honest with Dr. Bellamy, he'll get the help he's needed for a long time. And the parents and families of the girls will finally have closure." He tipped her face up to his and smiled. "Now, let's change the subject to you and me."

Margo smiled back. Now that she'd stopped asking for happiness for herself, God in His mercy was giving her what she needed.

Cole's dark eyes softened. "I need to tell you again how sorry I am for the way I handled things."

Margo smiled. "It took two of us to mess it up. I made bad decisions along the way, too."

"Well, now we have a chance to start a brand-new life."

"Yes," she said, feeling a warm glow. "We do."

He sighed and stepped away. "Unfortunately, I have to start mine now."

Mine? Another chill ran through her.

"I packed before I came over. I have obligations, Margo. It's not fair to keep asking other people to take up the slack." He smiled. "You have obligations, too. But you're definitely up to the task."

She couldn't speak. She could barely think. He was leaving for good? Their brand-new lives would be separate? Her hopes and dreams wouldn't be his?

Cole's brow furrowed. "Are you okay?"

Scrambling, afraid she'd cry, she summoned a broad smile. "I'm just surprised that you're heading back home tonight. It's nearly eight. You'll be driving in the dark."

He chuckled. "I have these really neat things on my truck called headlights. I'll be okay."

Get out, she wanted to scream. *Get out before I fall apart and look as stupid as I feel right now.* Margo turned him toward the front door. "I'm sure you'll be fine, but if you hurry you can make some of the trip while it's still light out."

He laughed. "Okay, okay, I'm on my way." He stopped in the open threshold, then smiled and kissed her softly. "Bye, Chief."

"Bye," she repeated, wondering how she could still be breathing without a beating heart. "Stay safe down there in the big city."

"You stay safe, too." He paused. "Know what? You're going to make a great leader."

She didn't watch from the doorway as his truck backed out of the driveway and headed south. She was too afraid she'd follow.

Slowly, Margo walked up the stairs to her room, grabbed her white terry robe and a dorm shirt, then headed for the bathroom. The Everly Brothers used to sing about doing their crying in the rain. She'd do hers in the shower.

It didn't help.

The first time they'd said goodbye the depth of her sorrow had been almost debilitating. But this…this was so much worse. Margo sank to the foot of her bed and turned to God again.

"I know I'm headstrong," she whispered. "I know I'm not perfect. And I know I said I'd never ask another thing of You if You helped me stop the killings, but—" She stopped and sighed. Because she couldn't break her promise. Not to her Lord.

Beyond tears now, she went downstairs and poured herself a glass of orange juice. She was putting the carton back in the refrigerator when she looked to her right and saw the small linen sampler her mom had stitched for her years ago. It was so familiar, she barely noticed it anymore.

The Lord Helps Those Who Help Themselves.

Margo swept off her robe and bounded upstairs to change, suddenly alive with purpose. A few minutes later, she was in her car and on her way. Her hair was wet, her sinuses would never be the same and no amount of makeup would cover her red nose. But he wasn't getting rid of her that easily!

Two hours later, she was being announced by the security guard and riding up to Cole's fifth-floor apartment in the elevator. Her stomach was a mess again. Her lungs were barely working. She watched the floor lights over the doors change. Three...four...five.

The elevator dinged. The doors opened.

And there he was. Margo rushed to fill Cole's open arms, her tears streaming again. "I love you," she sobbed as they held each other tightly. "Please say you love me, too."

"Forever," he whispered huskily. "I never stopped."

"Then how could you leave me tonight?"

Releasing her, he touched her cheek. "To give you time to realize that these past two weeks, working together, caring about each other again, could be the prelude to the rest of our lives."

"And if I hadn't driven here?"

"I would've come to you. And this time I would've waited until you were ready to be my wife."

Margo burrowed into his arms again as feelings of peace and contentment washed through her. "Please ask me again."

Smiling, Cole stroked her hair and tipped her face up to his. "I love you. Would you like to marry me? Soon?"

Sighing, thanking God for second chances, Margo waited for his kiss. "I'd like that very much."

EPILOGUE

The oaks, maples and pines in the churchyard were ablaze with color: deep burnished golds, vibrant reds and oranges, deep russets and greens, all glistening in the early afternoon sun. Margo smiled from the window of the children's Bible-study room. It was a perfect day. The chairs on either side of the white runner leading to the festively decorated white arbor were twelve rows deep and filled to capacity.

Everyone was seated. Friends, neighbors, Cole's mom and dad, and his brothers' wives and children...the Charity P.D. and their families...even Steve O'Dell had come back for the nuptials. He was working in Mercer County now, and seemed to be happy there. Somewhere beyond the arbor, Cole and his two brothers waited.

Jenna came over to her and smiled. "It's almost time."

"I know," Margo replied, suddenly short of breath. "I can't believe how nervous I am."

Laughing, Rachel joined them. "It's not too late to back out."

"Never. Never, never, never."

Jenna fussed with a few tendrils around Margo's face, and Margo smiled. Her two best friends looked radiant in strapless russet satin. Unable to choose one of them as maid of honor, she'd asked them both, and Cole had followed suit. His brothers were his best men.

She glanced around suddenly, her nerves increasing. "Where's my mom?"

Jenna checked the interior of the church. "I don't see her." Beckoning Rachel, she spoke to Margo again. "We'll go find her. But don't worry. Nothing starts until you're ready. Oh—and promise me you won't sit. You'll wrinkle yourself."

"I promise," she returned, crossing her heart—then catching sight of herself in the long, oval looking-glass Bridal Creations had dropped off earlier.

The woman in the mirror was a stranger. There were no lines of concern over her brow now, no black-and-gray uniform, no gun at her hip, no loose bun at the back of her neck.

Today, beneath a crown of white baby mums, pearls and ivy, her auburn hair fell softly over her bare shoulders. The bodice of her strapless gown was a miracle of tiny white sequins and seed pearls; the skirt was a bell-shaped flare of white silk. Long white satin gloves left her fingers bare for the wide gold band she would wear for the rest of her life.

Suddenly, she couldn't wait. She touched the tiny gold cross at her throat and thanked God for this beautiful day, and the beautiful man who was waiting for her. She and Cole had each had some growing to do this past year, and they'd come through it stronger than ever, and more committed to each other and their faith.

She looked toward Heaven. She'd done so much talking to God over the past few days, it was only fitting that she let Him know what was on her mind today.

"Lord, thank You," she said softly. "Bless this new life we're beginning. And bless the new career we've chosen."

They'd talked a lot in the past month and a half, and in the end, they'd made a decision that pleased them both. She'd left the police department in Brett's capable hands, and Cole had turned down the partnership job in Pittsburgh. In a matter of weeks, she'd have her P.I. license, and they would officially launch Blackburn Investigations, where their specialty would be reuniting families while they built a loving family of their own.

"With Your help," she whispered.

Laughing, Rachel, Jenna and Charlotte rushed into the room, her mom the happiest she'd seen her in months. The champagne-colored suit she'd chosen looked wonderful on her. Smiling, she came to Margo and kissed her soundly on the cheek. "Ready, honey?"

"Feels like I've been waiting for this moment forever. Yes. Yes, I'm ready."

Jenna put the cascading bouquet of white mums, pearls and ivy in Margo's hands, then kissed her right cheek.

Rachel kissed her left. "Be happy," she said.

"I will," she murmured, knowing that Rachel would've given anything to have her husband beside her today... just as Margo's mother would've loved for her husband to be here.

The lovely strains of "Edelweiss" began.

Rachel and Jenna picked up their bouquets and went to the doorway, and Charlotte McBride took her daughter's arm. "Honey, I prayed for this day."

"Me, too, Mom," she returned, smiling.

Then the music came up and Margo walked toward

the man she loved, her heart swelling with every step until, finally, she met Cole's warm brown eyes, and her mother placed her hand in his. Where it belonged.

* * * * *

Dear Reader,

It's been said that the Lord works in mysterious ways.
I've often wished I could understand those ways. Like
my character Margo, I've questioned why God doesn't
step in to fix things when life gets difficult. And I'm
ashamed to admit that, sometimes, I wasn't very nice
about it when I asked why this or that was happening.
Though it might sound trite, it took me a while to realize
that things happen for a reason. Maybe what we prayed
for wasn't the best thing for us at the time. Or maybe
dealing with stressful circumstances was a way to make
us stronger and wiser. Perhaps we simply needed to experience the bad to appreciate the goodness. I'm not sure.
What I know personally is that for every time I've been
disappointed, there were far more times when I've been
truly blessed. That's good enough for me.

Wishing you God's Peace and Bountiful Blessings,

Lauren Nichols

QUESTIONS FOR DISCUSSION

1. Torn between her love for her mother and her love for Cole, and knowing that they were both terribly unhappy, Margo made the only decision she felt that she could. She gave Cole his freedom and the opportunity for happiness with someone else—and remained with the mother who desperately needed her. Did she make the right choice? If not, what else could she have done? What would you have done?

2. Margo backed away from God after repeated prayers that went unanswered. Have you ever felt the same frustration and hopelessness she felt? If so, and you found your way back to God, what happened to make you trust in God again?

3. Why did Cole walk away after Margo told him she loved him but she had to let him go? Did he truly believe she was lying to him? Or was he simply separating himself from an emotionally painful situation? Was there ever a time when you walked away from a disturbing situation because you refused to see both sides? Did you regret it?

4. After learning the identity of the Gold Star Killer, Chief of Police John Wilcox couldn't allow the son he loved to go to prison. Instead, he thwarted the investigation and got his son psychiatric help. This is an extreme example of protection. What would you do, given the same set of circumstances, and why?

5. Margo takes the advice of her pastor and goes to Cole's unfinished home in the woods to talk to God.

She feels God's presence here more keenly, though they haven't been on speaking terms for months. She ends up railing at God in her frustration. Have you ever shouted at God this way? Did you regret it? Do you have a special place where you, like Margo, feel God's presence more acutely? Do you talk to Him the way you talk to a friend, or do you feel God deserves a more formal, respectful approach?

6. Adam has suffered with low self-esteem because of teasing and bullying, leading him to act out his anger in a far different way than other teens deal with the same problem. Did you experience similar problems growing up? If so, how did you handle it? Do you feel that bullying in schools is a more dangerous problem these days? How should it be handled?

7. Margo and Cole remained silent about their love for each other, afraid that speaking truthfully would result in their being hurt again. Have you ever been afraid to question a friend or family member about a painful emotional issue because you feared what the answer would be? If so, have you asked God for guidance?

8. At the beginning of their relationship, Cole's faith was lukewarm at best. He was a strong, capable, confident man who attended services because it pleased Margo. But when he lost her, his job and the potential for a life in the small town he'd come to love, he turned to God for solace. Did you feel this was true to his character?

9. It's not clear in the book why Steve O'Dell resigned his position in the Charity Police Department.

Sometimes, people can't talk about the things that are really on their minds. Why do you think he left? Was he angry at being passed over for the acting-chief position? Was he secretly in love with Margo, and knew she would always and only love Cole? Or was he embarrassed because Margo—a woman eight years his junior—censured him about sharing confidential police information outside of the department?

10. Do you know people who have a hard time sharing emotional problems, even with a trusted confidant? Knowing that they'd feel better if they shared their troubles, would you encourage them to open up to a friend or minister, or back off and let them handle it on their own?

LARGER-PRINT BOOKS!

GET 2 FREE
LARGER-PRINT NOVELS
PLUS 2 FREE
MYSTERY GIFTS

Love Inspired
SUSPENSE
RIVETING INSPIRATIONAL ROMANCE

Larger-print novels are now available...

Love Inspired.
HISTORICAL
INSPIRATIONAL HISTORICAL ROMANCE

Bestselling author

JILLIAN HART

brings readers
a new heartwarming story in

Patchwork Bride

Meredith Worthington is returning to
Angel Falls, Montana, to follow her dream
of becoming a teacher. And perhaps get to know
Shane Connelly, the intriguing new wrangler on
her father's ranch. Shane can't resist her charm
even though she reminds him of everything he'd like
to forget. But will love have time to blossom before
she discovers the secret he's been hiding all along?

Available in August
wherever books are sold.

**Steeple
Hill**®

LIH82841

www.SteepleHill.com